My Sister's Wedding

Dear Trish —
Thanks for having
me out here!

peace —

Hannah Goss

MY SISTER'S WEDDING

Hannah R. Goodman

iUniverse, Inc.
New York Lincoln Shanghai

My Sister's Wedding

iUniverse, Inc.

For information address:
iUniverse, Inc.
2021 Pine Lake Road, Suite 100
Lincoln, NE 68512
www.iuniverse.com

De Saint-Exupery, Antoine. *The Little Prince*. 1943.
Renewed in 1971 by Consuelo de Saint-Exupery.
trans. Richard Howard. 2000. New York: Harcourt, Inc.

New Order. "Bizarre Love Triangle." *Substance 1987*. Warner Brothers, 1990.

ISBN: 0-595-31265-9

Printed in the United States of America

For my daughter Chelsea and grandmother Bernice

Special thanks to:
my husband Michael and my parents Louis and Sheryl.

CHAPTER 1

The blue dress clings. It should hang. The ruffles droop. They should poof. The bright blue of the dress clashes with my late summer sunburn. I look like the American flag. Blue dress. Red skin. Blond hair. Not a good look.

I can't believe I have to wear this in public.

Maybe I won't go.

Maybe I'll pretend I have bad cramps, a fever, chicken pox or jungle rot. (My best friend Peter used to get that on his feet back when reveille jerked us awake every morning at Camp Chepatechet.)

Unfortunately, I can't cure my problems by slathering foot goop on them. First, Justin, my boyfriend, has decided to turn alcoholic on me. Second, Peter and one of my closest friends, Susan, are now dating. They have that kind of stuck-togetherness that all high school couples have right before they are about to have sex for the first time or when they just started doing it. It could be either one with them. Obviously I don't know. Even though *I* have been Peter's *best friend* since we were four!

Wait. Forget all my problems because today, Saturday, September 28th, the other alcoholic in my life, my totally hung-over sister, Barbara, is getting married to the "codependent enabler" himself, Michael Adler. (I learned "codependent enabler" at one of the Al-Anon meetings Michael dragged me to a few months ago). Although I wish I could contract some putrid infection that would prevent me from joining in on these festivities, I know that even if I had tuberculosis (Does anyone even get that anymore?), I'd go to the wedding anyway. After all, who's going to make sure Barbara's shoes match, her hair and make up are done, and, for God's sake, she makes it down the aisle? My sister is twenty-four. I'm fifteen. She's hung-over on the most important day of her life. I'm not. Who's really the older sister?

That's her now, throwing up in the bathroom next door. She got smashed last night at O'Malley's Tavern with fifteen of her loser friends from high school. They all still live at home, and none of them can seem to finish college or get a decent job. Okay, two of them work for "daddy," and my sister sells belly shirts at Twist at the Stanford Mall. That counts. I guess.

"Barb?" I yell toward the bathroom. "Everything okay?"

I hear a muffled noise that sounds like, "Yeah…I'm okay."

I pile my hair on top of my head. For a moment I'm a blonde Audrey Hepburn in *Breakfast at Tiffany's* (My grandmother, Bubbie Helen has gotten me into old movies). I try to ignore the blue glare of the dress my interior decorator mother, Bernice, picked out. Barbara and I refer to her as "Martha" (as in Martha Stewart). Of course the dress has a matching shawl and purse made of satin. "Martha" made these herself because the ones the dress shop had looked like "chintzy Wal-Mart garbage." And, of course, "Martha" wasted an hour arranging a bouquet of hydrangeas and white roses especially for me.

While my sister is so hung over she is having trouble getting ready for her own wedding, my mother is upstairs ironing the hem of the wedding gown for the fifteenth time and rehemming my color coordinating shawl because, "It's so crooked it will make me nauseated to look at it all through the ceremony!"

As I pin my hair, my thoughts jump back to Justin and Peter. What a mess. Justin may or may not show up at the wedding because he may or may not even be up yet. Peter will be there but Susan will too, so I really won't exist. Who will I hang out with at the reception? I hear the toilet flush and the water running. I push my own problems out of my mind again. I finish pinning my hair and reach for some cover up for the super size zit at the end of my nose. My puffy-eyed sister opens the bathroom door, flipping the fan switch on.

"I feel like shit," she proclaims. Our orange cat, Mensch, rubs his chin on Barbara's leg. She ignores him. I reach down and scratch him behind his ears and then push him away. Let's not have cat hair all over us on top of everything else.

And, Barbara, of course, doesn't look like shit. Except for her puffy, toffee-colored eyes, she looks, as usual, effortlessly beautiful. Perfectly shaped eyebrows she doesn't have to pluck. High cheek bones and a small straight nose. A totally zit-free face and coloring, even after hours of vomiting, just the right shade of peach and lips just red enough not to need makeup.

It's such a waste.

I take another quick glance at myself in the mirror. I'm too tall, too skinny, and too zitty.

But this isn't about me.

"Barb, we're running out of time. Let's just get your hair up and make up on so we can get you into your dress," I say, trying not to respond to her drama. She's famous for those productions. Take last night. Before she went out with her loser friends, she spilled champagne on the white outfit that she was wearing to the dress-rehearsal dinner. She just had to "have a little taste of that fabulous bubbly" Great Uncle Sid dropped off when he got into town with his third wife, Tess, whose fake boobs are the only things that don't shake when she speaks. Anyway, she had spilled it all over her and started to cry, screaming, "I screw everything up. I'm not going to the stupid dress-rehearsal dinner. I'll just screw that up too." My mother and father were already gone, so I helped her find another dress. Her response to my assistance was, "Thank God for you, Maddie. You're so together." I felt like slapping my forehead like some drama queen myself and saying, "Do I have a choice?"

Anyway, now she is checking her breath by blowing into her cupped left hand. It's time to get moving and she's worried about her bad breath? Her dress has about twenty-five tiny buttons and a bustle. She wanted to be "girlie and traditional" Ha! I have to get that girlie and traditional butt into that complicated dress.

"Do I smell?" She walks over to me and leans forward.

I'm 5'8" and she's 5'2". So all I inhale is her freshly washed hair, which smells like apples.

"No," I say, and she really doesn't, which I find amazing. I grab a brush and steer her into my desk chair in front of my full-length mirror.

"How am I going to get through this?" she asks, as I brush out the tangles in her damp hair.

"You just are," I tell her.

"I feel pretty crappy right now. I guess if I need to barf, I'll just puke into one of those huge containers of flowers by the aisle." She sounds gleeful at the idea of making Mom mortified.

"No freaking out Martha today," I say. Sometimes I feel better about Barbara when we make fun of Mom together. Like last night, Mom insisted that we all wear blue "because we are special members of the family." She had my father in a light blue shirt with a light blue-and-white striped tie. She bought me a blue-and-white striped dress and for herself, a blue silk shirt and skirt that had white-striped banding all around the hem and the cuffs. When Mom pulled my striped number out, Barbara was standing behind her in the living room, rolling her eyes and putting her finger down her throat. Then she said to my mother, "I think we should all just go in jeans. And to make you happy, 'cause you're into this whole blue-and-white theme, we'll all wear white tank tops." My mother whirled around and looked at her like Martha Stewart would look at Puck from *The Real World San Francisco* after he picked his nose and wiped it on his tee shirt. I shook my head at Barb and mouthed, "Stop," but I was laughing too. It's dysfunctional, but it's how we bond.

"You'll be perfect," I say as I finish her hair and she grabs the foundation from the nearby bureau.

She puts tiny dots of rosy beige cream all over her already even complexion. "Maddie," she says. "What will I do without you?"

I shake my head and take the foundation back, giving her the under-eye concealer. This, she actually needs.

All I can think as I watch her smear the concealer under her eyes is, "You'll have to manage. I'm done."

My sister wanted a very small wedding, which really pissed Martha off. My mother has an office in Manhattan. She's done interior decorating for famous people like David Letterman. She never met him, only his live-in girlfriend. She also decorated a couple of soap opera actors' apartments. A few were on my favorite soap, *All My Children*. She's a legend in town, and I think she really took it hard when Barbara announced her plans. No elaborate, lace-and-chiffon table skirts or place settings. No showing off to the rest of her yenta friends to say, Maybe my screwed-up daughter can't get into college or get a real job, but, look, she's having this great big expensive wedding and marrying this perfect, nice, Jewish doctor.

Eventually, my sister caved. One day, a few weeks after Michael and Barbara got engaged, Barbara sat in the living room with a bunch of wedding magazines scattered all over the light blue-and-gold oriental rug. She chewed her nails and ripped out pictures of dresses, table settings, and flower arrangements, even wedding bands. She didn't seem to be enjoying herself. Patience is not one of her virtues, and I think you need patience to plan a wedding. At the moment my sister made her aggravated noise: "Ahhhhrrrggg!" my mother wandered into the room. "How's the planning going?" she asked. I was lounging on the couch, reading *Seventeen*. I peered up to watch the drama unfold.

At first my sister was stubborn. "Fine, mother. I'm doing fine."

My mother played it cool. "Okay. Well, good luck."

My sister was still chewing her nails but had her thinking face on. Crinkled brow and scrunched nose.

My mother was half way to the kitchen when Barbara said, "Listen, I'll let you do this. But I have to have some say."

My mother squealed and she's not a squealer. They compromised on a small ceremony (just relatives which turned out to be 55 people) with me as maid of honor and her friend, Lori, a bride's maid and a large reception (about 150). Mom was thrilled and Barbara was glad to be rid of the extra hassle of planning a wedding.

This whole planning of the wedding thing has been a total nightmare and my sister, who used to be an I-can-pull-it-all-together-when-I-want-to drunk and even, at times, a nicer-than-the-sober-version-of-herself drunk, has now become a mean and ungrateful, nasty drunk. She orders me around and expects me to cover for her all the time. She used to be bitchy sometimes. Now she's a bona fide bitch.

At her high school graduation, when I was ten years old, Barbara couldn't get up for the brunch my mother had planned at our house. I rolled her out of bed. Got her in the shower. Sat her in the tub while I turned the shower on. Two years ago, for my Bat Mitzvah, Barbara was MIA two hours before we had to be at the temple. Michael called me on our private line to say he couldn't find her. He thought she was with Jen Conrad (one of those loser high school friends) the night before and she hadn't called him. Or maybe she was with Lori Cecci? Had she called home? He wanted to know. Had she come home? Could I tell everyone she had a crisis at work (at Twist?) and would meet theme at the temple? At the time, I was just like Michael, the whole "lets fix Barbara" thing, and so I said, "Of course. Absolutely!"

But now I have seen the light with Barbara and even with Michael, who by the way is nicer than Tom Hanks. For a while he was the one saying we have to save her from herself. We have to stop covering up for her. In February, after a drunken Valentine's dinner at Clemente's where she started to do a strip tease for him at the table, he said to me when I met him in the basement to sneak her upstairs, "Maddie, it's time to do something about Barbara. What if I hadn't been with her tonight? She could have been raped. I have to do something."

A few days later he dragged me to an Al-Anon meeting and even talked about doing an intervention. But then, he blew it. He got this nutty idea. If he got Barbara to marry him, then she'd "settle down", and everything would stop being crazy.

He was wrong. And now I get it, but I'm the only one who does. I didn't understand the problem until the Al-Anon meeting. The leader, a four hundred pound grey-haired woman who wheezed the whole time she spoke, said, "People who cover for alcoholics are really just as much of a mess as the alcoholic. Because stop and think about this: Why are you covering up for them? Don't you realize that by covering up for them, you're contributing to the problem? You're enabling them not only to drink but to walk all over you. What does that say about you?"

I don't think Michael heard that part. But I did. I didn't understand everything. But one thing I got was that covering for Barbara was a bad thing to do.

Even though in my head I see a flashing neon stop sign, I can't seem to stop covering for Barbara. Last night, she got so wasted her friends called me. They wanted me to be there when they snuck her in through the basement. Then, I had to undress her and make sure she was breathing and then put her to bed. I wasn't surprised to find myself doing this at 2 a.m., the night before her wedding. But I was surprised to feel annoyed. That was new. I used to just do it and not really notice how I felt.

I'm not sure why Barbara's so screwed up or why we all seem to be so careful around her. When Barbara arrived at my Bat Mitzvah brunch two hours late, with mismatched shoes, large black sunglasses and only drank black coffee, my father put his arm around my sister and said quietly, "Long night?" as if she had been up all night writing a term paper. My mother told people that Barbara hadn't been feeling well lately, and then gently steered her into the ladies room, took off the shoes and put some makeup under her eyes.

No one ever says she's almost twenty-five and has never held a real job. No one says she dropped out of college and partied high school away. I remember the car ride home from the brunch. We all made excuses for her. None of us mentioned that she was hung over. My father said to my mother, "Barbara has her priorities screwed up. She should have been there on time."

"She doesn't have priorities." My mother sounded tired.

They were silent for a moment and I volunteered. "It's okay. At least she came."

My mother turned around and patted my leg, "You're very sweet, honey."

My father sighed. "Barbara is just a free spirit. She can't be tamed."

Now my mother sounded annoyed when she replied, "Well, I think she's immature. A late bloomer. Eventually, she'll have to grow up."

Eventually still hasn't happened.

My sister has one true talent, and it's actually an amazing one. She can sketch and paint. She tossed around the idea of art school at one time and constantly sketches in this journal she carries around. I mean, the thing that gets me is she's really smart, obviously good at getting people to do what she wants, and very talented. So why has she let her life turn to crap?

Sometimes I wonder if her craziness has to do with my father. My parents married sixteen years ago when Barbara was eight. My mother was married before, to Barbara's father. It's a complicated story. My parents have only given me bits and pieces. My mother's mother, Bubbie Helen, has filled in the bigger pieces of the story.

Three years ago I asked my Bubbie Helen to tell me the whole story. One night during Christmas Vacation, when Barbara and I went out to California to visit her, she did. It was a really cool night, and we sat on her front porch drinking iced-coffee. Barbara was already in bed.

"Your mother was married to a "putz". It wasn't good. She left him after a year of marriage and nine months pregnant. Even though she was only nineteen, she refused to be a victim." Bubbie paused and took a long drink of coffee. Then she continued. "So, she moved back home and decided to go to college and study art history. I had only been widowed one year, so I was happy to have the company." Bubbie teared up. "We were very close." She quickly wiped her eyes. "I was Mom's Lamaze coach."

"So how did mom meet Dad?" I asked, intrigued with the vision in my head of young, pregnant "Martha".

"Two years after Barbara was born, Bernice met your father in Central Park. Your mother and Barbara were eating hot dogs. Barbara started to choke, and if you can even believe this next part: your dad, a thirty-two year old bachelor, raced over and grabbed Barbara and administered the baby Heimlich on her. After it was determined she was okay, your mother (who was very shy) invited him to stay and have an ice cream with them. He hung around and played with Barbara all afternoon." Bubbie looked far away as she told the story.

"Then what happened?" I asked her.

"Bernice and Stan didn't exactly fall in love there. They actually became friends for about two years. I couldn't figure out their relationship. Every Sunday, he would come over for dinner. I just loved having him over. He was intelligent and funny. A real character. Making us watch wrestling on TV. Cooking underdone pancakes on Sunday mornings. Then lecturing us on the importance of Physics. He made your mother very happy. But it didn't seem romantic to me. He seemed like her buddy. I just think your mother wanted their relationship to be private." Bubbie was on a roll now. She had a really peaceful look on her face. I just sat and listened.

"Sometimes he took care of Barbara when Bernice would have a late class. Stan and Barbara became so close over those years that Barb started to call him Dad. When your sister was eight, your parents married. You were born one year later. It was the highlight of those years. You were an easy, happy baby and everyone loved playing with you." Bubbie turned and looked at me and suddenly didn't look as peaceful. "Let's go to bed."

That story makes me think my parents must really love each other. When they argue, it's mainly about Barbara. My mother plays "bad cop" while my father plays "good" cop. Mom will say, "Don't stay out too late" when Barb goes out. Or she'll say, "Don't you want to do something with your life?" when Barb sleeps until 3 pm on her days off from Twist. If my father's around, he'll say to my mom, "She's young. Let her take her time to figure out her life." Or he'll tell Mom, "Barb is a grown up. Let her live her life the way she wants." I don't know what Barb feels about all of that. Once, in private, I heard my dad say to Mom, "We can't make her grow up. She has to do that on her own." My mother didn't reply.

❋   ❋   ❋

"For God's sake Barb, the waste paper basket was right next to you!" My mother screams from the bathroom. "Did you have to vomit all over the $700 veil?"

We are in my mother's bedroom and Mom is in the bathroom furiously scrubbing the veil in her sink and screaming every profanity possible. Barbara is standing in her dress bawling, makeup running. I am holding the bustle up with one hand and wiping Barbara's face with a tissue with the other hand.

"Sorry Mother, I guess I missed!" she spits back at her.

I am tired. Tired of my mother getting upset over the wrong thing. How come she doesn't say: "For God's sake. Barb, did you have to get trashed the night before your wedding?"

Instead we stand around screaming and crying over a veil.

Moments later, after I tuck Michael's ring (designed by his father who owns a swank jewelry store in town) into my tiny, blue-beaded purse, we tumble into the white stretch limo and are on our way to meet Michael, my dad, and Michael's parents at the temple. We are fifteen minutes away. My mother is discussing draperies with the limo driver (she constantly tries to recruit more customers, no matter the situation).

"Now, Mrs. Hickman, my wife wants to buy all these curtains and pillows. I tell her: You make it! Why do you have to buy them? Women used to make this stuff. Why does she have to buy it?" says the limo driver, who is a balding, wrinkled man with a toothy smile.

"George is it?" My mother asks him. He nods, teeth gleaming. "George, your wife probably is a busy woman. She takes care of you and maybe the grandchildren—"

"Great grandchildren!" He announces as if they were a prize.

"My!"

"Six!"

"Well, then, George, don't you see how hard she works?" George nods vigorously. "Does she really have time to make drapes and pillows?" She stresses the word "drapes". My mother refuses to say curtains.

"I guess not." Poor George has been defeated by Martha.

"Let me give you my card...."

My sister and look at each other and roll our eyes. She mouths to me, "Sucker!"

My sister busies herself with her compact, fixing her lipstick. It all somehow doesn't seem real; my sister is getting married and leaving the house. It just doesn't seem possible.

My mother closes the deal with George and turns back to us. She looks over at Barbara and says, "Did you bring any concealer?"

"Why?"

"Because you have circles under your eyes."

I stare at my mother. And that's because...?

My sister looks into her mirror. "I already put some on."

"Well," my mother smoothes her dress. "You need more."

"No, I don't, Mother." Barbara turns to me. "Do I need more concealer?"

I stare at her, not wanting to get involved. Not wanting to open my mouth for fear that I may scream, who gives a shit! You're friggin' hung over! Can we just say it already?

I say nothing because now they are going at it. I tune them out and stare out the window. I have started to become aware of my family and how screwed up it is.

Luckily, I have been gone for most of the summer. I was a CIT at Jonah's Rock—this "artsy fartsy" camp as my mother so charmingly referred to it. I have been going there since I was eleven. Bubbie sends me every year.

"Why don't you want to intern in the city at Cousin Hilda's modeling agency?" she asked me all last year.

"Mom," I had told her. "I don't want to work for a modeling agency. I want to be a writer. I'm finally old enough to be a CIT for the Pub Shop."

"What, in God's name, is that?"

I had felt so frustrated with her. "It's the publishing hut where kids get on computers and type out stories, poems, and plays. I get to be a counselor to other kids who want to write. It's a great opportunity."

I was not about to do some stupid fake internship with stupid bulimic and anorexic models hanging around.

"But the agency is well known and would look so good on your college transcript." She so desperately doesn't want me to turn out like Barbara.

I knew I'd have to sell this to her. "This will look great on my transcript for NYU. I know that many of my counselors went to school there."

Mom couldn't knock NYU. She caved.

Bubbie started sending me to Jonah's Rock when she found me writing my first short story in the sixth grade. It was about a girl whose father died and her mother won't cry about it. At the end the girl tells her mother, "It's okay to cry." And the mother does. "We should cultivate her talents," Bubbie had told Mom. That was back when they were talking to each other. My mother never really said much about the camp until she came up one parents' weekend when Erica Jong happened to be reading some of her poetry. Erica Jong is some feminist who writes, according to my mother, "smut." Mom saw this lady and recognized her. She grabbed my father and me and marched us right out of the Pub Shop, muttering, "Pervert!" All the woman was doing was reading some harmless poetry about fruits and vegetables. Speaking of fruits, my mother is nuts.

Bubbie lives in California, and I visit her for two weeks every summer and for Christmas vacation. Other than that, I don't see her. She and my mother haven't really spoken since I was about ten.

A couple of years ago I talked to mom about Bubbie right before I left: "Why don't you come?"

My mother threw me a dirty look and said, "Helen and I don't get along and it has nothing to do with you." The way she said that to me made me feel like I had just scraped my fingers over a chalkboard. I never asked again.

We used to have Bubbie come for all the High Holidays when I was little, and my mother would be so mean to her the whole time. That one year when I was ten, Bubbie brought my mother a bottle of wine wrapped in this really shiny red and silver paper and a basket of mangoes and coconuts she had brought back from a trip to Hawaii. My mother took the bottle of wine and threw it out. Then they started to argue:

"How could you bring this into my house?" My mother's voice was low and angry.

"Bern, what's the big deal? People bring wine as gifts all the time. So I'm forbidden from bringing a gift to my daughter and her family?" Bubbie's voice sounded light.

There was a long silence at this point. Then Mom said in the same low voice:

"You promised you'd never do this again. Get out of my house."

And that was it.

For a year after the wine bottle incident, Mom would only let me talk with Bubbie on the phone. She never told me why. I went out to see Bubbie again. But no explanation was given for the year I didn't see her.

The thing is I have a lot more in common with Bubbie than with my mother. Bubbie is a writer—although when I say that she says, "No, I'm not. I just write." Years ago, she found God at a "Sufi Camp" and she suddenly felt the urge to write and couldn't stop. She has been writing poetry ever since. Sometimes I wish she were my mother instead of old Martha Stewart. Bubbie pays attention to who I am. She doesn't want to make me into something, and it totally sucks that she won't be coming to the wedding.

The wedding.

Deep breath.

We're here.

CHAPTER 2

"Hava Nigila! Hava Nigila!"

I am standing in the corner of the reception room in Temple Shalom. People are running in circles, flapping arms and legs. I'm trying to smile. My sister is in the middle of the circle hopping up and down and two fisting champagne. Her dark long hair swings as her gown swishes around her ankles as she chants and sings. She is the only person who doesn't look like a fool while drunk and dancing the Horah.

Michael stands close to her, clapping, chanting, and grinning. It's sad. He has convinced himself that marrying him is going to make Barb better. When he and I were in the middle of the circle, swinging each other around and in between smiles for the camera, I whispered to him, "Barb was hung over this morning. Do you really think she should be getting tanked now?"

"Hey, Maddie," he said. "It's her last time. Now that she'll be living with me, she won't be able to drink."

What could I say? I left the circle. I just can't pretend tonight.

Plus, Justin hasn't shown up yet, and I'm beginning to wonder if he is coming at all.

I wander down the hallway to the pay phones, past Rabbi Shapiro's office and down toward the two classrooms where I spent many a Monday, Wednesday, and Sunday sitting in Hebrew School, chanting prayers, memorizing my haftorah for the big event—the Bat Mitzvah.

If it hadn't been for Peter, I would have spent elementary and junior high school embarrassed about being Jewish. Not only did the kids call me "bagel", but I wanted to play baseball or Power Rangers instead of Barbie and house.

As we grew up together, we discovered Woody Allen movies and thanks to my father, the World Wrestling Federation (before it became World Wide Wrestling Entertainment). One weekend when we were in fifth grade, my crazy father took us to Madison Square Garden to see Mankind and Stone Cold Steve Austin, Hulk Hogan and The Rock. Peter's dad disapproved, but Mrs. Shaw is the kind of mother who says, "Go ahead, but don't tell your father." We left carrying big foams hands with the index finger protruding and letters across the knuckles that said "Hulk is number one!", and my dad took us to McDonald's for cheese burgers and milk shakes.

"My dad's going to kill me!" Peter said with glee. Mr. Shaw is a health food fanatic.

"Don't tell him," I advised.

Dad passed him a burger. "Dig in, son."

Not only did they bond over the junk food, but also my dad's a scientist and Peter loves science, so they bond over everything from El Nino to the Laws of Thermo Dynamics. Just last week Peter came by the house to watch the PBS special, *El Nino: Fact or Fiction.*

The hallway is freezing. Near the phone sit glass-enclosed cases of Jewish memorabilia. Antique stars of David, Menorahs, and—oh wow—there's the Shabbat candlesticks we made. Peter and I were uninvited to the last services back in seventh grade because we got a little out of hand. Mrs. Blinish—who we called Mrs. Blemish because she had a big wart on her chin with a hair growing out of it—had assigned us to make candles. I mean four-year-olds make candles. We were thirteen, about to be Bar and Bat Mitzvahed.

Anyway, I dripped wax all over the rabbi's office because I really enjoyed peeling it off when it dried. But I got some on Rabbi Shapiro's chair and tried to scrape it off with a letter opener and scraped off some paint. The rabbi came in just as I had peeled it off.

He was a fat, hairy, loud man. "What are you two doing?" he bellowed.

"I was just trying to decorate your office for Shabbat," I stammered. "It's a, um, a tradition that I read about."

He ignored me and glared at Peter. "Do you know about this tradition?" he asked Peter.

"Yes, sir," Peter lied, sweat beading on his forehead. "We read about it in *Shabbat Monthly.*"

"I've never heard of that magazine."

"That's because it's new." Down the sweat rolled.

Rabbi Shapiro glared some more. "Clean this mess up and then copy the first five pages of Genesis in Hebrew."

At the pay phone, I decide to call Peter before I check on Justin. I want to delay the inevitable: finding out Justin can't make it to the reception.

Peter's mother answers. "Oh, Madeline! What a lovely ceremony! We're just about to leave for the reception. We had to come back for the gift because you-know-who forgot to put it in the car! Men! Anyway, we are coming and—oh, you looked just beautiful in that dress. It was a little puffy as you had said, but you were a knockout!" The lady likes to talk.

"Thanks, Mrs. Shaw. Is Peter coming with you?"

"Yes, and that Susan too." She sighs. Susan's only half Jewish, but I think mainly Mrs. Shaw doesn't like her because Susan is an obnoxious, stuck-up brat most of the time. I can't tell you how many times I have been fed up with her. When we were twelve, she kept saying, "My house is bigger than yours and my daddy makes more money than yours." Last year, when I wanted to take Peter to a WWE match for his fourteenth birthday, Susan said, "That's such trash. No one we know watches wrestling. We're going to the *Phantom of the Opera.* I already got tickets."

Yet, every time we get into a fight and I decide I will never speak to her again, Susan calls me, brings over homemade chocolate chip cookies, or, God, brings me flowers to apologize.

But she's a loyal pup. When we started middle school, all the popular girls decided I was "too Jewish" for them.

"You're all prejudiced," Susan told them. "Not to mention stupid."

"Jew lover!" they yelled back.

But she stayed by my side and sat with me at lunch and hung out with me at recess every day year.

Mrs. Shaw interrupts my thoughts. "Oh, and Maddie," she says. "Mrs. Mallano called me and she said Justin wouldn't be coming to the reception."

I'm silent.

"Maddie, now come on." Mrs. Shaw sighs again. "Things have been tough for him since his father died. He just needs some time." She didn't know the half of it. Justin is staying home because he has a hangover. I say goodbye and lean against the wall.

Justin's dad dropped dead at work while he was making a routine walk through his plastics company's factory. At the funeral, I just kept squeezing Justin's hand. He wore a navy suit and didn't cry. My parents came, even though Mom disapproved of my romantic relationship with Justin. She thought he was too wild because he liked to skateboard and wear baggy clothes that showed his boxer shorts. Plus he had an earring. "Very unkempt!" she always says. Fine for a friend but nothing more. But since Justin's father died, my mother calls him "Poor Justin" and invites him and his mother to dinner sometimes.

I wonder why Mrs. Mallano hasn't noticed Justin is sick only after a late night out. I really like his mom, especially since before his dad died, she was on his case if he was even ten minutes past curfew. But since they had to sell the company, she says nothing, even when he doesn't come home all night.

Justin started to drink a lot after the company was sold. Our weekends together revolved around parties and beer. Peter and Susan would come with us sometimes, but it wasn't really their thing. It wasn't mine, either. I stuck with him because he can be really dumb and crazy when he's drunk. When you love someone, you sometimes do things you don't like. That must be why Michael convinces himself that Barbara will be okay. I guess I have been doing the same thing with Justin. At first I told myself his father just died and I should understand his going a little crazy. Now, I'm not sure what I'm doing with him.

At Chris "Burnout" Burns's party in June, Justin drank twelve beers and decided that it would be fun to pee into empty beer bottles. Susan and Peter were with us, and while Justin hopped through the dingy, dark basement in search of places to make his deposits, they were making out in a corner. I stood around holding Justin's shoes and pants because he had decided bare-assed and barefoot was the way to go. Eventually, Peter and Susan stopped making out and noticed Justin's antics.

"He's such an alcoholic," Susan said in a matter-of-fact voice.

"He's such an idiot these days," Peter said. "He just wants to impress upperclassmen."

I stood next to them and the three of us watched Justin trip over a chair and fall on the floor, laughing and peeing.

Peter grabbed my arm and whispered, "Let's go, Maddie. Let's walk home. Justin won't even notice."

That was the last party we went to together.

I feel sad that it will be Peter, Susan, and me at this wedding without Justin. Even though it's been hard to talk to Justin lately, maybe I should call him and see if he's okay. I put another quarter in and dial.

"Hello?" It's Justin's mother.

"Hi, Mrs. Mallano, it's Madeline."

"Hi, sweetie," she sounds tired. "The momser got in late and is a total mess. I can't promise you he's coming."

Whenever Justin has been out all night she calls him "the momser," which is Yiddish for idiot.

I burst into tears.

"Madeline, come on now. You can't let him ruin this special day."

"But it's not special if he's not here."

"Stop this. You go and enjoy your sister's wedding. Justin will be fine. But he's in no shape to be at the wedding. You know how he is after a late night. He won't be good company."

I sigh. She is right. What I don't understand is, how does she deal with him? What does she say when he comes home drunk off his ass? "Well, just tell him I called."

When I hang up, my hand lingers on the receiver almost as if holding onto the connection would help Justin. Finally, I let go. There's nothing I can do about Justin. He's not coming.

I turn around and bump smack into a six-foot, green-eyed, Freddie Prinze Jr. look-alike.

"Oh—Oops! Uh—sorry, I was just trying to uh—" he stammers. Only the waiters had on white jackets and black ties like his. "They're looking for you. You're the sister of the bride? Right?"

"Yeah?"

"Well, I heard your mother and father saying, 'where is?'—I mean, I didn't get the name, but I saw you leave the reception and figured, well, you're in a bridesmaid's dress so they're probably talking about you."

"Thank you. I'm on my way back in."

"Wait a minute—"

I hesitate. "What?"

"Your last name is Hickman? Little Maddie—my sister used to baby-sit you!"

"Huh?"

"Angie is my sister. Angie Dunay. I'm Sean."

Oh my God! This boy used to make fun of me for climbing trees and not playing Barbie. Angie used to bring him over when she had to baby-sit. "Oh yeah, I remember her. I think I remember you." I always thought he was only a year or two older than me, but now he seems more than that.

"You probably don't want to. I don't think I was very nice back then." He blushes the color of the Merlot Barbara likes. "Wow, you look a lot different."

"Well." Yeah, I have a huge zit on my nose.

"You should give me your number. Maybe we can hang out sometime."

I drop my shawl and then step on it and feel myself slide to the ground. I mumble, "My number's in the book," and scramble back to my feet. Then I stumble back to the reception.

CHAPTER 3

I haven't seen Sean in two hours, even though I have made my partners dance close to the kitchen door, hoping he will come out with more food or dessert or something. But maybe I was hallucinating. I'm so desperate and sad about Justin that I'm making up new boys that like me.

"Madeline, you really look beautiful!" Mrs. Shaw says.

Mr. and Mrs. Shaw, Peter, Susan, and I are nibbling from a table of chopped liver, knishes, brisket, lox, mini bagels, and gafilta fish. Peter and Susan are feeding each other pieces of bagels smeared with cream cheese. He licks cream cheese from her thumb, and they smile like people with a secret. I stop mid-chew. I want to throw up.

Instead, I ask Peter's father to dance. Peter and Susan have floated onto the dance floor, where they cling together like two overcooked pieces of spaghetti. Even my mom and dad are pretty hot and heavy. I want Justin here, holding me. The band moves from the "Horah" to the "Macarena." Mr. Shaw giggles and spits out pieces of ruggala. I take his hand and we join the crowd of wiggling hips and arms.

I feel suffocated, excuse myself, and head for the bathroom to escape. Sean is sitting by the coatroom reading. Will he think I've tracked him down? I tiptoe past, hoping he won't notice me and hoping he will.

Without looking up he says, "Uh, hey!" His face is beet red. "I…uh…that was really lame to put you on the spot and everything. It's just that I was watching you in the reception and you really looked unhappy. I made that up about your parents. I just wanted to see if you were okay."

How can someone who hasn't seen me since I played with Matchbox cars notice I'm totally unhappy, and my own best friend and my family haven't once asked if something is wrong? For six months I have moped, sulked, and cried. Why has no one noticed? Two words: wedding and sex. My sister's wedding has distracted my family, and sex has distracted my best friend, Peter.

I want to tell Sean the truth: My life sucks. I feel invisible. But I don't want Sean to think I'm a total Prozac case, so I look down at the book he's reading. Oh, my God, it's the best, greatest book of all time, *The Little Prince* by Antoine de Saint-Exupery. I almost cry.

"*The Little Prince*." I can barely get the words out.

"Well, uh—I know this is, like an eighth-grade book but—

"Oh, there's so many messages in it," I say. "You have to read it—

"—again and again," we say together.

"The fox and the whole thing with taming," Sean says. "It's—"

"—so true!" I finish.

"Yeah," Sean says. "The fox asks the Little Prince to tame him because—"

"—he wants a friend." I finish his sentence for him again. "And the Little Prince wants a friend, and he says that if the Little Prince doesn't tame him then—"

"—he'll just be like any other fox in the world." Sean rushes on. "And the Little Prince will be like any other little boy—"

"But if he tames him," I chime in. "then they…they have a relationship, they mean something to each other, to the world."

"It's like the whole point of living is to tame each other, to need each other," he says.

We are both breathless and flushed. I feel dreamy and far away from the wedding, until my mother comes barreling out into the hallway:

"Madeline Hickman!" She throws an obnoxious, snotty look toward Sean. A mere peasant, a waiter. "Madeline! What are you doing out here?"

Everything matches perfectly with the blue motif: pearl earrings, necklace, and bracelet. Nails, lips, and shoes all pearl white.

"I'll be right in, Mother," I answer sharply.

"Well, hurry. Your sister wants a couple of final pictures before we head back to the house." She casts another nasty look at Sean and turns smartly. Her heels click as she leaves.

I look back at the magic. Sean is just some random episode, not a special connection. My bleak life returns.

"Well," I avoid looking directly at Sean. "It was nice to see you again." I turn as smartly as my mother did, which horrifies me, and rejoin the reception.

CHAPTER 4

Back at our house, Peter and I are in my bedroom without Susan, who went home to change. We stand by the window that overlooks our *Home and Garden* backyard and watch our parents and the Adlers, Michael's parents, laugh and drink ice tea. My eyes move between looking at the family and the oak tree that's taller than our house. Peter, Justin, and I used to climb it when we were younger. Lately, I have had the urge to crawl up inside its huge, thick limbs and take a nap.

"Are you okay?" Peter asks.

I don't say anything because I'm not really sure where to begin. It's hard to choose between "I miss my best friend" and "I'm worried about all the alcoholics in my life."

"Maddie, I know you're worried about Barbara. She's going to be fine. Michael can take care of her now."

I feel flushed with frustration. "Gee, Peter, that really makes me feel better." I know I sound like a bitch, but I can't really fake anything any more. I have done all the smiling and hiding I can for today.

Peter puts his arm around me. "You have to stop trying to take care of everyone."

"What do you mean?" I sound defensive and cranky.

"You've spent your whole life taking care of Barbara. You've been doing the same with Justin. I just think you need to stop…You know…" he says.

I feel like he has punched me in the gut. Peter and I go way back—our mothers were in a playgroup together with a bunch of other Hadassah women. I was the loud, obnoxious one. Peter was reserved, a dork with a big mop of brown hair and thick glasses. He looked like Cousin It. I was the opposite—blonde, no glasses, not to mention tall, awkward and skinny. My mother insisted that I keep my hair long, even though I always had it up in a baseball cap. The first day of fourth grade I wanted to find out what would happen if I poured glue all over my hands and let it dry. Peter wanted to do whatever I did, so he tried it too. But he was nervous, and his glasses kept slipping down as he tried to keep his hands under the desk and put the glue on them. When he pushed his glasses up for the millionth time, he smeared glue all over his nose and face and in his nappy hair. Fat Mrs. Cagle screamed and told us to leave the classroom. Peter cried.

By the time sixth grade rolled around, Peter, Justin, Susan and I were like Siamese quadruplets. Susan and I were on softball together, which she hated. I was a Pop Warner cheerleader with her, which I hated. Justin and Peter played baseball and football together. Justin quit when his father died last year. Soon after, Peter traded both in for debate team and student council.

Now, I push Peter's arm off my shoulder. "Do you have any idea," I say, "how hard it is to just watch people you love destroy themselves? No, you have no idea, Mr. Perfect. Mr. Perfect Grades. Perfect Girlfriend. Perfect Family. Give me a break."

"You don't have to lash out at me, Maddie. I know you're upset. I'm just trying to be your friend." Peter's face is peaceful, placid. It drives me nuts.

"You are such an ass!" I explode and move to the other side of the room. "Justin has been our friend since fourth grade. Doesn't that mean anything to you? If I started to drink or take drugs, would you just drop me? Is that the way friendship works with you, now that you and perfect Susan are humping each other? If everyone else isn't as perfect as you and Susan, then you just say, 'Oh well! The hell with them, they aren't perfect like us.'"

"Jesus! First of all, Susan and I are not humping each other. Second, you're going crazy over this." He pushes up his glasses. "Friendship doesn't work that way with me and you know it. Susan and I—I mean—I did not stop talking to Justin because he drinks. I stopped talking to him because he stopped being Justin and started being 'too cool' for me. You were there all those times last year, remember? Justin would say to me, 'Hey, come on Peter, don't be such a pussy, have some beer, smoke some pot with me'? And then ditch me because I wouldn't do it." Red blotches appear on Peter's face. His glasses slip back down his nose.

"Yeah, I was there. But he needs help. He's hurting. He lost his dad and he can't deal with it. Have some compassion, Peter." I ache from missing Justin. His smell. His hands. His face. I don't want to give him up.

We look at each other.

"Anyway," Peter says, "you already have a new boyfriend lined up."

"What?"

"Sean Dunay. I saw you talking to him at the wedding. Didn't he torture us when his sister babysat us?"

The moment with Sean seems years ago.

I move back to the window and look out at my tree again. The urge to climb my tree is strong. I feel like crying. "Peter, I think you should go join our parents outside. I'll be out in a few minutes."

"Maddie, I'm sorry if I made you upset. It's just because I care about you and—"

"Just go, Peter, please."

He sighs. "Okay. If you need me or Susan just come get us."

Yeah. Now that would be helpful.

CHAPTER 5

When school got out last year, Susan, Peter, Justin, and I did a rerun of the past seven summers; for the three weeks before I left for camp, we spent our days at the beach and our nights at Holiday's, a mini-golf, bowling alley, movie theater, and arcade complex in town. Everyone from school showed up there. It is the only place in town for kids to go, especially freshmen. Ninth graders almost never get invited to upperclassmen parties, so this is where most of us hung out.

Even though we were still doing the same things together, now we were two couples rather than four friends. Susan and Peter were really into each other, making out with their tongues visible and rubbing each other's thighs while they waited their turn to bowl. Justin and I were definitely together, but when we were with the group, we didn't hold hands or kiss or anything. That was separate. So this whole lovey-dovey stuff embarrassed us. Susan started to get on my nerves more than usual. She had always been a little outrageous and outspoken, saying things like, "That color makes you look like a cancer patient" or "Wow. New haircut, hmmm? But it looks a little like one of those mullets from the eighties." But we all loved her because she is sassy and hilarious. Once when we were at the arcade, a bunch of older, scummy-looking boys hit on us, ignoring that we were with Peter and Justin. Susan said, "Maybe all the acne on your face has clouded your vision, but we have boyfriends." They were so embarrassed they just walked away. It definitely pays to have a friend like Susan at times like that.

But soon, each night at Holiday's, I stopped wanting to play mini-golf with her (and Peter) or do anything else with them.

"Petey?" (She called him this once they moved to make-out mode.) "Do you want some of my fries?" Susan tilted her head and pouted her lips, like giving him a fry was giving him something girls do only in pornos.

"Sure, sweetness." (That was his nauseating make-out mode name for her.) Then she leaned over his lap, dipped a fry in ketchup, and "accidentally" missed his mouth so she smeared ketchup all over his lips.

"Do you want me to get that for you?" She proceeded to lick the ketchup off. I was practically puking into my Dr. Pepper. Justin mumbled, "Shit, man...gross."

"Petey" was just as bad. He fed her gummi bears, spent hours trying to get enough tickets from games to win her a stuffed animal, kept his hand on her butt while she played scooter-ball. They were so sickening, so embarrassing, that Justin and I didn't want to be around them. We would all go to the arcade and then split up. It used to be that if we ever split up, Justin and Peter always headed for the video games and Susan and I played mini golf.

"Come on, Preppie, I'm beating your ass. Let's go," Justin would say to Peter as they played X-Men together.

"You better calm down, you flannel-shirt-wearing freak." Peter would say as Justin slapped and banged the machine. "Your pants will fall off if you keep jumping around like that."

Now Justin sulked and glared at Susan and Peter as they played their cutesy, cuddly-wuddly games. Often he would say, "They're just babies anyway. We need to start having some real fun." Then he would drag me to some party that had alcohol, where I sat in a corner while he got blitzed.

I realize now that his father's death amplified Justin's problem. The first time he got drunk was at the beginning of freshman year. We went to a party and after an hour, I couldn't find him. I finally interrupted Susan and Peter's make-out dance routine among the many teenage bodies moving slowly in the basement of I-don't-know-whose house. "Hey, guys, have you seen Justin?"

They managed to untwine themselves from each other. We found Justin half an hour later in an upstairs bathroom, draped across the toilet with his head cradled in his arms.

"Justin." Peter nudged his shoulder. "Come on. We have to get you sober before we go home."

We got a ride from one of the few not totally smashed Seniors to the Dunkin' Donuts less then a mile from home. Peter spoon-fed Justin black coffee and kept saying, "You're going to be all right," while Justin mumbled over and over, "Thanks, man." Susan and I sat together silently watching the two of them. We didn't get home until two in the morning. What was weird was that his parents said nothing. I didn't even drink, and I was grounded for two weeks. When his father died in late January of that school year, Justin got really depressed. Then in February his mother announced she was selling the company, and the nightmare began.

❧   ❧   ❧

Justin's father had died three weeks before, and I was in Justin's room. His head was in my lap and he was just looking at me and playing with my hair. We were listening to the soundtrack to *Say Anything*. We were both obsessed with eighties music and movies. *Say Anything*, *The Breakfast Club*, and *Pretty in Pink* were our favorites.

We started dancing and making out to "In Your Eyes" by Peter Gabriel. At that time, he would hold me or kiss me without a word. It was sort of nice at first, but it was starting to get creepy and not-Justin-like. Deep down, I knew he needed to talk and the silence probably wasn't a good thing. But every time I said something like "Justin, are you okay?" he would only kiss me fiercely or hug me tighter.

So he was gripping me and kissing my neck and then kissing my mouth. I was confused with his smell and the feelings of our bodies so close. I forgot that his fervor and silence weren't good things. I forgot that his passion was not so much because he "loved" me as because he didn't want to think about his father. But this time I felt wetness on my shoulder as he stopped kissing me. When he pulled away and looked at me, he was crying. I touched his eyes and his cheeks, and I took the corner of my tee shirt and wiped his face and nose. He started to cry harder. I murmured, "I'm sorry Justin, I'm so sorry—"

Now that I look back, maybe he was finally about to cry for his father, but then his mother called from downstairs. "Justin!"

We stopped dancing. Justin rubbed his eyes and turned the CD player down.

"Yeah?" He was still rubbing his eyes and straightening his clothes.

"Is Maddie staying for dinner?"

He looked at me and I nodded. "Yeah."

"Okay…Justin, come down here for a minute."

"But, Ma…."

"Justin!"

He grinned at me and said, "I'll be back in a minute. Get naked and meet me in bed." He was back to the old Justin.

I punched his arm and laughed. "You wish." Then I grabbed his hand and said, "We can talk later." He kissed my hand and left.

I closed the door, picked up the CD cover for *Say Anything*, and read the lyrics even though I had the songs memorized frontward and backward. A few minutes later Mrs. Mallano called, "Madeline, why don't you come down."

Her voice sounded the way it had when Justin's father died, the same tone.

In the kitchen, Justin was at the table with his head in his hands. Mrs. Mallano was stirring soup with one hand and dabbing her eyes with a Kleenex with the other one. She turned to me.

"What's wrong?" I looked at Justin.

"I just got a call from Charlie," Mrs. Mallano said. "He's made an incredible offer on the business." I sat down next to Justin and put my hand on his shoulder. "I—I can't afford to keep it any more. It's too much upkeep, and I don't have time to juggle that and my real estate work." She stopped stirring and banged the wooden spoon against the pot. Justin hunched his shoulders. "I feel awful about it, but I'm constantly schlepping myself from my office to the company. All they need me for is bookkeeping. I don't know how to do the business the way your father did. He was the business when he was there. Everyone worked better, harder." She sighed and pushed her bushy hair out of her eyes. "It will go bankrupt if I don't sell it. I know Joey would want me to save it—to sell it to Charlie and John." They were Mr. Mallano's partners.

Justin slammed his fist down. I jumped. Mrs. Mallano almost knocked over the pot of soup.

"Justin, Justin! Now, I have got to save it. I have to sell it—"

"Goddamn you! You're so selfish! You don't love dad. You don't care. That's all we have left of him. Doesn't that matter to you?"

Her expression went from pain to hurt to anger. "Now you listen to me. I loved your father with everything, with everything! With something you cannot even understand. It matters to me, it matters that I cannot do it all—save the business, save your father—that I couldn't be there when he died. That I couldn't save him." She was shaking and trying not to cry.

She raised her chin. "I'm your mother, and I'm the parent and grownup here. I make the decisions." Her eyes flashed. "Listen to me carefully. This is hard not only for you but for me. I have to do what is right for us. Not just for you."

She dried her eyes, rubbing them, as upstairs Justin had rubbed his. "You two go up and wash for dinner." Justin glared at her for a few long moments.

When we came down from the bathroom, we had a normal dinner, as if nothing happened.

Mr. Mallano was loud and booming. When Mrs. Mallano once forgot to pick up his shirts at the dry cleaners, he slammed his fist on the counter and told her all she thought about was herself, just like Justin. I never liked Mr. Mallano; he was too big and too bossy. Justin didn't like him either before he died.

Now in my bedroom, I hold a picture from last summer. Justin is tickling me. He didn't think I knew he was drunk. It wasn't until his father died, I realize now, that I could see he was his father's son.

I put the picture down. From the window, I watch Peter and my father, who sit next to each other in green Adirondack chairs. Dad turns toward Peter and waves his hands as he talks. I smile my first real smile of the day. They could be discussing anything from the laws of thermodynamics to China, the female wrestler. Michael's parents stand nearby, with what is probably iced tea in their glasses—not booze. Why do they seem to love Barbara so much? Maybe they see her as a good-time, carefree girl. Maybe they think she's good for their introverted son. Who knows? People probably wonder why I'm with Justin.

CHAPTER 6

❀

It's 6:30 Monday morning and I'm in the bathroom brushing my hair. My spectacular zit has nearly disappeared. Will Sean call? I wonder. Do I really want him to? Will Justin even acknowledge what happened this weekend? Will things ever go back to normal?

The phone rings. Brush in hand, I run back to my room. "Hello?"

"Hi." Justin.

"Nice of you to show up Saturday." I slam the brush on the bureau.

"Maddie, come on, you know I'm sorry."

Familiar words. "Oh, yeah, I forgot. This is the part where you apologize and promise it won't happen again, and I, like an idiot, believe you."

"I'm sorry. That's all I can say."

Silence.

I want to throw it in his face that Sean Dunay flirted with me. But instead I do what I always do. I start to think about Justin's feelings. He's been going through a lot. I have to be patient with him, or he'll think I don't care. "Look, I know you're sorry. I just wish you'd been there."

"Me too."

"I had to resort to doing the Macarena with Mr. Shaw."

"Oh? Should I be worried?"

"Yeah…unless you can make up for it Friday."

"Friday?"

"Family dinner with the in-laws and the Shaws."

"Are Preppie and his girl going to be there, too? Maddie, I don't know."

"Justin—"

"Okay, okay. I'll be there."

"What happened Saturday?"

"I'll be over in a few minutes. We can talk about it later."

"Sure." I hang up the phone and stare at my reflection in the mirror over my bureau. I look sad.

❦   ❦   ❦

As Justin and I walk past Peter's house, I think back to when we all used to walk to school together—Peter, Justin, Susan, and I. At the beginning of this school year, we stopped. There was no discussion—it just ended abruptly. Now Peter walks a mile out of his way to get Susan, and then they go to school together. Peter and Justin are down to polite nods to each other if they both happen to be at my locker.

Now, Justin takes my hand. The weather is still hanging on to summer; it's about seventy-five degrees and no wind. "So, what did happen on Saturday?" I ask him. "Everything was fine Friday night. You went to the rehearsal dinner. Then you went home. You went home after, right?"

"Yeah...well, actually, I stopped by Jim Shay's party." He pauses and he rubs his head, like he does when he knows he's done something wrong. "I guess I overslept, because Mom was gone when I woke up. It was already pretty late, like two or three."

"You were hung over." Lately I have started to say out loud what I see Justin doing. It was sort of funny to me that I could be this up-front with Justin and never say "drunk" or "hung over" to Barbara. I just keep holding her hair while she pukes. It seems easier to tell Justin he's drinking too much. This whole thing is hard to understand.

I stop walking and drop his hand, then wait until he looks me in the eye. "That's why you missed my sister's wedding? Because you had to drink until you passed out or peed yourself or—"

"Maddie, I just overslept. It's no big deal." He grabs my hand and starts to walk fast, dragging me.

"No." I shrug away from him. "You were trashed. You were hung over."

"No, I just overslept," he yells and walks ahead of me.

"I think you were hung over," I say softly.

He turns around and parrots my voice. "I think you're wrong."

"I think you're a liar!" I shoot back.

"What the hell am I lying about?"

I feel like screaming. Maybe being up front about this isn't doing any good. Okay, I will be calm. His blue eyes look a little watery and sad. I still love him. Why? "You know Justin, this is really ruining everything with us." I speak quietly, proud that I'm not playing my usual drop-the-subject, be-kind-to-Justin game.

He walks back to me and replies in a low voice, "You're letting it ruin everything."

I stare at him. How he can blame me for his stupid crap?

Before I can say anything, he switches back to sweet Justin. "Hey, look, I'll be at your house on Friday—and no drinking."

I brighten a little, but I'm still annoyed that he blames me for his own problems.

"Promise," he says.

I will give this another chance. Maybe Justin can stop drinking.

Maybe.

❦   ❦   ❦

"So, Justin, how are the grades this term?" my mother asks, delicately wiping the corner of her mouth with a celadon green linen napkin.

Justin swallows a massive amount of mashed potatoes. "Well, I'm passing everything."

Barely.

"Well, that's a start!" my father says, winking at me. I say a silent *thank you* to my always-on-the-sunny side father. He has a big blob of mashed potatoes on his left cheek. Martha frowns fiercely at him and stabs at the corner of her mouth. My father takes the hint and reaches for his napkin.

Michael's parents take tiny bites, and in between they smile or nod, depending on if someone is talking. Mr. Adler never says much. Usually it's Mrs. Adler who does all the talking. And once you get her going, she can go on and on. "How's school for you, Maddie? Are you still writing for the literary magazine? My cousin Jody's daughter is the editor of her school literary magazine. Well, she's a senior though. I bet it's a lot of work—"

My mother interrupts. She has to, or Mrs. Adler would talk right through the next several courses. "She had straight A's spring quarter and won the Freshman Annual Writing Contest." Mom beams at me. "We are so proud!" The only nice things my mother says about me are about school. I happened to have a good fourth quarter last year. That was before Algebra II.

My father smiles at me through a bite of roast beef. "That's right, she's our resident poet."

Mom sips some of her red wine. "Oh, well, that's just a hobby. Maddie is also very good at math and science."

I am? I look at Justin, who squeezes my hand.

"I think you'll make a fine doctor some day, actually." Mom slices a piece of meat with her freshly polished Sterling silver knife.

A doctor? God no! What is she talking about?

"Maybe you'll get to finish the degree your sister started," she says, resting her knife against the china plate.

What degree? She never even got past the first year. My father forces a cough. I shift in my chair. The Adlers stop smiling. My mother is about to attack my sister, and she isn't even here to defend herself.

"Bern," my father says, keeping his voice light. "Barb never wanted to be pre-med. She wanted to go to art school."

"Well, apparently she didn't do either one, did she?" my mother snaps back at him. Was my sister pre-med in college? What's up with that mystery?

Before I can ask, Mrs. Adler pipes in. "This roast beef is excellent!" She nudges her husband, who nods and smiles, and I feel embarrassed. I have barely touched my food as it is, because this type of dinner is usually uncomfortable. The conversation almost always goes the same way, except Barbara is usually here to defend herself. "I'm working on trying to figure out what I really want to do," she might say now. "It's just taking me some time. Besides, I work hard. I pay my bills." To which Mom usually replies, "Not all of them. We pay your food and rent." My father or Michael will intervene before it gets worse. "Boy," one of them might say, "this food is delicious." Or Michael will tell a story about what happened at the hospital that day, or my dad will talk about a student who tried to cheat on an exam or turned in someone else's paper. Anything to break the tension between Mom and Barbara.

My mother, at this point, decides to attack me. This, too, is typical. First she builds me up, and then she shoots me down.

"Madeline, eat. You're looking too thin."

Justin looks at me with sad eyes. He seems to know how much I hate this. A warm rush of understanding flows between us. I forget about the wedding and him at home passed out.

He takes a stab at the conversation, trying to smooth over the tension. "Mrs. Hickman, these potatoes are awesome!"

My mother's usual clenched expression softens. "Thank you, dear! Does your mother cook much for you? It must be hard for her."

Forget smoothing over. His expression changes and darkens. My mother busies herself with her napkin.

I reach under the table to grab Justin's hand, but it is limp as a wet sock.

❧   ❧   ❧

After dinner Justin and I take a walk. Our house is set back into the woods, so we first head down our forever driveway. We are silent. The sun is low in the sky, and it is dark under all the trees. In the dim light, he looks calm, his face soft, and the dark expression gone. I take his hand and direct him toward our favorite make-out spot, a big oak with long, sweeping branches. You can hide behind the trunk; it's so thick no one can tell you're there. I lean against the tree. Within seconds, my hands are under his shirt and his hands are under mine. We are breathless from kissing and balancing ourselves against the tree. All of the sudden, he pushes me hard against the tree and tugs on the zipper of my jeans. This is the off-limits zone. We have never had to discuss it. We both know it.

"Justin."

"Yeah?" He's working hard on my jeans. My hands go down to pry his fingers away.

"Justin, please." I start to feel all passion and warmth drain. The sharp points of the bark stab into my back. "What are you doing?"

"I just want to—" He slides a hand down the back of my jeans.

"Please." I'm scared. "Stop…"

Forget this! I dig my fingernails into the hand still working on the zipper. "Ow!"

I push him away. He's not that much taller or bigger than me.

He sucks on the back of his hand where I apparently broke the skin. His eyes narrow into black slits. Then he spits out, in this small cold voice: "You bitch!"

I feel tears well up. "Justin—"

"No! No! I have been the good boyfriend. I have played all these little make-out games for months. We aren't just friends any more, Maddie. We're, like, together. This is what you're supposed to do!"

"Oh, even if I don't want to!" I spit back. Hot anger has burned up the tears.

He starts to laugh, reaches in his oversized jeans pocket, and pulls out a tiny bottle of Jack Daniels. He breaks it open and laughs. Then he drinks and laughs again.

"Oh, okay, now this is the answer, Justin." I gesture at the bottle. "This is it. This solves all your problems."

"Yeah, well it makes me forget about my hard on."

I bite my lip and shake my head. What happened to where we were at dinner? The understanding and comfort I felt? "Why do we suddenly have to do it?"

He laughs again and drinks the whole bottle down. Walking back toward the driveway, he throws the bottle down and laughs again and again. Then he turns to me. "That's what's so sad. I've wanted to do it this whole time. You just didn't know it." He heads down the driveway away from the house. Away from me.

"Justin!"

He waves his hand at me as if I were an annoying fly. I give up and watch him go, feeling pissed off and everything all at once, like I just failed a test I studied so hard for, and the teacher won't let me take it again, even though I'm a good student. Helpless and disappointed.

As I approach my house, my father's laugh booms out and dishes clink as my mother clears the table. I suddenly want to talk to Peter.

I miss Justin. I miss Peter. I even miss Susan.

CHAPTER 7

I spend Friday night crying and rereading love letters from Justin. One from last year makes me want to blast Sinead O'Conner's "Nothing Compares to You" and howl at the moon. *"Dear Maddie, The way you make me feel is like nothing else... When my dad died, if I hadn't had you there with me, I don't know if I would have made it... You make me feel like I'm not such a loser... I love you times infinity."* It kills me that he could be so loving and then such a jerk. Why can't he always be the sweet Justin? The one who needs me and makes me feel like a princess?

Saturday morning I lie in bed in my purple tee shirt, a birthday gift from Justin, and stare at the ceiling, remembering all the nights on the phone we talked for hours about life and what we want to do. Justin wants to be a professional skate boarder—Tony Hawk is his idol. When MTV had a special on him, we watched it together over the phone. Every few minutes Justin said, "Wow...man, that's what I want to do." We always watch TV together on the phone. Our favorite movie is *The Princess Bride*. Whenever we argue, he gives in by saying our favorite line from the movie: "As you wish." Every time it's on TV, Justin calls me and tells me what channel it's on, and we stay on the phone to the very end.

I sigh and look out the window. My tree's forest green leaves blow in the gentle wind. I look up at the clear blue sky. My shirt twists as I turn to look at the clock. Beside it stands a small gold-framed picture of Justin on his skateboard. You can't even see his face, just see the top of his head as he reaches down for the board to hop onto a curb. I feel a lump fill my throat.

My clock radio blinks seven o'clock. I'm sure my father is still asleep, and my mom is up and in the basement finishing her morning treadmill jaunt. My hand grazes one of Justin's letters and the tears start up again. It's a letter from when I was at camp just this summer. We had been apart for four weeks. *Maddie, I cannot wait for you to get home. We have so much to talk about. Stuff we can't discuss in letters because it is too complex, ya know? I miss the way we talk. I miss your voice and your beautiful face. I miss just kissing you and how we would kiss for hours and hours. I could kiss you forever.*

What is so amazing about Justin, what really gets me right in my heart, is that he seems so rough and casual on the outside. It's hard to believe that underneath the spiky hair and ragged jeans, he's so caring and loving. That's what attracts me. He's so complicated. At the last dance of eighth grade, before we officially started going out, we were sitting together on the cafeteria tables watching Peter try to ask Susan to dance. He stood in front of her, shifting his weight from foot to foot, holding out a cup of soda. She had her arms folded and was giving him a smirk that said, Are you going to make the move or not? Justin elbowed me. "Look at them. Their uptight asses are made for each other." A few minutes later, they were dancing, and Peter flashed us a thumbs-up. Justin shook his head and laughed. Then he turned to me and said softly, "Let's dance. I really want to dance with you."

He's the "bad boy." Bubbie always tells me, "Just don't let him be bad to you." She also told me to read this book called "Good Woman Who Love Bad Men." She said Justin may not be the "bad man" yet, but I should get myself informed of the profile.

Today is a good day to check the bookstore, because Dad and I are going into the City. Every second Saturday, we follow the same routine—take a long jog around Central Park, then go to Barnes and Noble and get a bunch of books and magazines. Dad usually gets a WWE magazine and a pile of science fiction books. I normally hang out at the self-help section. I own three copies of *Codependent No More* by Melodie Beattie and realize I'm definitely the "enabler" with my sister. I actually help her to continue to drink because I don't let her get caught. I keep covering for her. Three days before the wedding Barbara was supposed to pick up Aunt Sadie at the airport, but it was 7:30 in the morning and she still wasn't home from a night at Raffy's Tavern. My mother, fresh from her morning treadmill run, was making her way to Barbara's room to wake her up.

I intercepted her. "Morning, Mom. Do we have any of that fresh pineapple juice from yesterday?" My mother can always be distracted by a request for her homemade juice.

"Yes, sweetie. In the fridge. I've got to wake up your sister so she doesn't miss Sadie."

"She's already gone, Mom. She left fifteen minutes ago. She was worried about traffic."

"Really?" Mom adjusted the pink sweatband that matched her pink stretch pants and pink tee shirt (ironed of course).

"Yeah, she wanted me to tell you."

Mom looked at me, squinting her eyes. "Did she take her cell phone? Maybe I should just call her—"

"Oh, she didn't tell you? Her cell phone is dead. Something's wrong with it. Don't worry, Mom. Barbara will be fine. She had the sheet of directions you gave her." One lie after another.

My mother looked out the window behind me and said, "Madeline, her car is outside—"

"Don't you remember? Michael said he'd drive."

As soon as my mother went upstairs, I rushed to the phone and called Michael.

"I just totally lied to Mom. Barbara never came home, and she's supposed to pick up Aunt Sadie. We have to do something. I told Mom you were with her. Maybe you can go get Sadie, and I'll call her friends. She left her cell here so—"

"Damn." Michael sounded more tired than angry. "All right. I'll get Sadie. Call me in the car if you find her."

"If we don't find her, then we'll tell Mom you dropped Barbara off with Aunt Sadie at her hotel. We'll say that she's helping her settle in. Mom will love that." It is amazing how I can find ways to cover and lie. I can make anything work.

I finally found Barbara at Lori's house. She waited until Michael got Sadie and then he picked her up. To this day, no one knows what really happened.

So reading *Codependent No More* hasn't stopped me from enabling Barbara. It's made me more depressed over her, though. I was going to give her a copy, and I considered giving it to my parents. But, that itself is codependent. Anyway, what would be the point, since they don't realize Barbara drinks too much? Or if they do, they don't know what to do about it. How can parents be so out of touch with reality?

Dad and I have been going into the city on Saturdays since I was a kid. (I used to roller skate while he ran, until I got tall enough to run with him.) After Barnes and Noble, we go to H&H Bagels and get one of their soft, fresh, hot bagels. Barbara has never joined us because she is usually working or sleeping off a hangover.

I suddenly realize that I'm waking up on a Saturday morning without worrying about Barbara. Usually Friday nights are the worst for her drinking, and Saturday mornings meant a major hangover. She often slept until noon, if she could. If she had to go to work, I woke her up around seven so she could pour down tons of coffee and start to dry out. I feel free, and it's a good feeling.

As I brush my teeth, I wonder how she's doing. In the week since the wedding, we have had only one phone call—from Michael, who said they were having a ton of fun. I wanted to ask him how Barbara is, whether she's drinking, but my parents were in the room. I'm glad she's his problem now, but is she getting really hammered? Maybe she isn't. Maybe Michael is right. Maybe because she's away from us, she's happier. Maybe she's so happy she doesn't have to drink. Maybe.

Dad and I finished our four miles and are taking turns at the water fountain near the west entrance of Central Park.

"MADDIE! HEY, MADDIE!"

Susan.

My father lets out an annoyed sigh. He tolerates Susan for my sake, but he can't stand her parents. "They should have stayed on Long Island," he said once. Her dad, Marty, is a dentist who wears plaid all the time and calls me "Maddie Mo" for some reason. Her mom, Elaine, is a first-grade teacher who wears huge bows in her hair and weighs at least three hundred pounds. But the main reason my father can't stand them is because they ask embarrassing, inappropriate questions. My mother disagrees. "They have character, Stanley," she tells my dad. She invited them to my bat mitzvah, and over cocktails, Marty asked my father, "So, how does it feel to have your only biological daughter bat mitzvahed?"

Who else would be moron enough to make a point of Barbara's not being Dad's natural daughter?

Anyway, today it's only Susan and Elaine.

Now Dad rolls his eyes at me before he wheels around to greet them. "Hello, ladies!" He can turn on the charm when necessary.

"Hello, Stanley!" Elaine has this incredibly obvious crush on my father. She comes mincing toward us, floppy red bow flapping in the breeze. The Gellers seem to think that because Peter's family and we are the only Jews in the area, we are all friends. We are all part of this club or something, like a Jew Crew. I know I sound awful, and sometimes I feel bad about making fun of them with my dad. After all, Susan is my friend, but her parents can be pretty embarrassing.

"Hi, Maddie!" Poor Susan. Her mother looks like an overripe cherry—red everywhere: shirt, tennis shoes, and shirt. Susan looks nothing like her mom. Well, not yet anyway. She wears conservative clothes, maybe to be as different from her mom as she can. Today she has on tan shorts and a kelly-green shirt with a collar. Marty is a "miser," as my father says, but Elaine wants Susan to have a dresser full of pleated khakis and navy button downs. It's like Michael and Janet Jackson—you can't believe Elaine and Susan belong to the same family.

"That's so great you run, Stan! Keeps you in terrific shape!" Elaine touches my father's arm.

It takes a lot for me not to yell, "You could run too!!!"

"Are you guys off to H&H?" Susan asks.

I start to tell her we already ate. "Actually we—"

Elaine beams at my father. "You two deserve a real breakfast. Let's go to that fabulous Greek diner on eightieth."

Off we go. My father sends me an apologetic look. But I understand. If you throw any sort of greasy food at my dad, he'll eat with you no matter who you are.

Although my father is a somewhat religious Jew, he gave up eating kosher around the time he and my mother got married. He won't allow some things in our house: bacon or pork. Bubbie has said to me, "I think your dad feels less guilty abiding by some of the rules, but the truth is—kosher is kosher. Being a little kosher is like being a little pregnant. It just doesn't work."

At the diner, Alex, the owner, cooks my dad up a plate of nonkosher delights, cheese and sausage omelet with bacon on the side.

"This is such a lovely looking meal." Elaine is babbling and gazing at my father across the table. "I certainly never eat this kind of food. I'm always so careful about what I put inside my body. You know what they say, your body is your temple. But just once in awhile I like to be bad, and oh, how I love chocolate chip pancakes and home fries."

My father nods and shovels bacon, omelet, and toast into his mouth, probably thankful that my mother isn't here to make him stop and wipe the grease from his face.

It is quite a sight.

Susan, on the other hand, is very quiet—unusually quiet. I realize that Dad is engrossed in the food and Elaine is engrossed with Dad, and suddenly I want to talk to Susan like I used to—about Justin. Before, I never had anything but good things to talk about. But now I'm desperate, and really, I have no other friends. I already know what Peter thinks about Justin and me.

Before I can say anything, she whispers across the table, "Let's go to the ladies' room. I have to talk to you."

We go into the single-stall bathroom. She closes the door and turns around with dramatic flourish. Then she blurts out, "We did it. Peter and I had sex last night. It was at his house. His parents were gone all night, and we did it in his bed. We had been planning on doing it soon, so we had the condoms…"

I get this giant lump in my throat. I feel like Susan just slapped me across the face. I feel like someone told me Peter *died*. I feel my heart break. I feel alone.

But she's still talking and she wants to share this moment. You know, I think if this had happened just a little under a year ago, I would've had a better reaction—maybe.

"Maddie? Maddie?"

I nod my head and manage some sort of listening noise.

"I know we should've waited—because after all, we'll get married some day. But I love him so much that—

My feelings must be visible because she interrupts herself. "Oh, God, Maddie! Here I'm and—well, *Justin. You* guys aren't even together." She pauses awkwardly.

I know that Susan does not mean half of the obnoxious things she says and does. Usually I can see that and see Susan. Right now, I can't.

"You know what Susan? You're so selfish. Can't you—for once—see outside your own little world?" I'm seething and hurting all at once. I glare at her and stomp out. I think my father is psychic, because he's already paying the check.

Before Dad and I go home, we stop at Barnes and Noble and I head straight for the self-help section and grab *Good Women Who Love Bad Men* and, as a backup, *The Art of Letting Go*. What's so great about my dad is that when he sees the titles of the books, he doesn't say a word about them.

CHAPTER 8

❀

The self-help books don't help. It's Sunday morning and I feel like a dirty piece of gum stuck under someone's shoe. I'm the used Kleenex that litters the side of my bed.

Susan popped my bubble. The bubble that's been protecting me from feeling so alone and sad. I wish Barbara were here. At least I could focus on her and feel useful. Plus, she would give me some great advice like, "Screw those idiots. You don't need friends like them. And get rid of Justin. He's a pain in the ass since his father died. I mean, I know it sucks, but he shouldn't take it out on you." Barbara isn't a member of the Justin Mallano Fan Club. She used to like him until he started to be a jerk, standing me up and not showing up when he said he would. Sometimes when he'd call she tell him, "You better straighten up or I'm going to kick your ass." He'd laugh, but she was dead serious. It's weird when Barbara jumps to my defense. She does pay attention to me sometimes.

The thing about Barbara and Justin is that they are so much alike. Both couldn't focus enough to do well in school. Both are creative and good at non-traditional things, him at skating and her at painting. When he came over, he'd skate to our house because he lived so close.

"Hey, punk, show me some new tricks," Barbara would say. She'd go outside and watch him slide, Ollie, and flip. "He's pretty good," she'd tell me.

Once he said to her, "Hey, Picasso, why don't you paint something awesome, like me?" And she did. She took my picture of him skating at the skate park in Darien. When she showed him, he flushed. "Wow, man, cool." She gave him the picture right before she got engaged. It's the only picture he has hanging in his bedroom.

Barbara never knew about Justin's drinking, because by the time he really got going, she was engaged and no longer had time to take us anywhere. I wonder what she would tell me if she knew? Would she say his drinking was no big deal or would she say he had a problem? Would she, maybe, talk about her own drinking? Who knows?

This morning my mother is at some luncheon with a client. My father is cutting the grass with his new Honda tractor mower. I'm a lonely ghost wandering through my house overwhelmed by memories. I float from the floral, lacey, pastel pink living room to the small, forest-green library off the kitchen and back to my own room—the only white walled room in the house. Finally, I arrive at the top of the basement steps.

I once had to sneak Barbara in through the basement when my father had fallen asleep on the couch down there watching *Smack Down*. I kept my hand over her mouth and guided her through the back door and past him, both of us trying not to laugh. She put her hand over my mouth at one point, and it was totally silly; the two of us with our hands over each other's mouths, half dragging each other up the stairs.

We all used to play Play Station in the basement and watch teenage eighties movies. When we were in middle school, sometimes Barbara would come in late, and we'd all be there playing *Legend of Zelda* or something. We assumed she was doing what all older sisters and brothers did, come home late smelling of beer and cigarettes. It seemed normal. We would giggle at how she'd stumble through the room, tripping on our shoes and bowls of potato chips. It seemed innocent.

Now, I leave the top of the basement steps and go through the kitchen, through the dining room, and then through the French doors that lead to the manicured gardens outside. God, Susan and Peter had their first kiss here one night last year when we played Truth or Dare, and I dared Peter to kiss Susan—on the cheek. His tongue was down her throat. I was so happy for them—and relieved. Now maybe Justin would take the hint. Of course, he didn't. At least, not that night. The next night, Justin and I had our first conversation here about being a "serious" couple.

It was ten o'clock. We had been outside playing Manhunt with all the neighborhood kids and decided to hide together in my back yard, knowing that no one would bother checking here because my house was set way back from the street. We sat on the glider in the middle of my mother's rose garden.

"Can you believe last night? Peter was totally tonguing Susan," Justin said.

I pushed the glider gently with my foot and sat sideways, looking at him, but he wouldn't look at me directly.

"Well, it was about time. They've been wanting each other for awhile," I said.

"Yeah, well, they should thank you, because you're the one who dared them to do it. I don't think Pete had the guts on his own."

I couldn't help what I said next. It came out before I could think. "I don't think you have the guts either."

He looked at the ground, and I saw red creep up his neck.

When he didn't say anything for a whole minute, I started to feel shaky and not sure if I had said the wrong thing.

Finally, he looked at me. "No, I don't have the guts to do that, but I do want to tell you something."

I waited, breathless.

"Maddie, I like you. I mean, I *like* like you. I want us to be more than friends. When we're in your basement, watching TV or playing video games, and we're all close, I just want to—you know—. And last night, I wanted to kiss you. You have no idea how much I wanted to." He looked at the ground again.

I leaned over and turned his face up to me. "So do it."

And he almost did. He put his face close to mine and whispered, "I'm too scared."

"Why?" I was whispering too, dying to kiss him right then.

"I don't know." Then he got up and started jogging around the garden, picking some of he roses and putting them behind his ears and singing a really old New Order song, "Bizarre Love Triangle": "I feel fine and I feel good/I'm feeling like I never should./Whenever I get this way,/I just don't know what to say/Why can't we be ourselves like we were yesterday." As frustrated as I felt, I was sort of relieved, so I got up and joined him.

Now, I sit on the swing crying. It isn't only the memories of Justin and Barbara. Peter isn't there for me to talk to anymore. Now that he's slept with Susan, what am I going to say to them? I imagine a conversation. "Hey, let's go play mini golf." "Um, no, we want to go have sex." I guess Justin is right. That's what you're supposed to do.

Everyone *does* do it. I know lots of kids who are sexually active, no big deal. Only, now that it's right *here*, I feel all messed up. It's like everyone is going to Paris and I wasn't invited—maybe I'm just too scared to fly.

Back inside, I sit by the window in the kitchen and watch my father. I pet Mensch, who's curled in my lap, while Dad rakes the leaves off the lawn. His jeans are brown with dirt. He turns around and waves to me. I wave back. A few minutes later he comes through the mudroom, pausing to stamp his feet and brush off the dirt from his jeans before coming inside.

"What are you doing home? I haven't seen you home on a weekend since you were eleven. Where's your crew?"

I burst into tears. Mensch leaps off my lap and runs to his food bowl.

"Madeline?"

I shake my head. I can't speak.

"Are you hurt?" He hurries over to me and puts his hands on my shoulders, inspecting my face to see if I'm in pain.

I shake my head and put my hands over my face.

He steps back. "You know, you've been very quiet since yesterday morning. I knew something was wrong after breakfast." He snaps his fingers. "Something happened between you and Susan. Of course! That snotty little girl. She's always got something obnoxious to say. It was yesterday, right?"

I wouldn't cry like this in front of my mother. It's too messy for her when I cry. The last time was in sixth grade when I came home from a Pop Warner dance. John Frizone had kissed me on the mouth with his tongue. I was mortified and grossed out. I threw myself on my mother's reupholstered Waverly print couch. All she said was, "Please don't wipe your nose on the couch. Go get a Kleenex."

Dad's different. Every time I'm upset, I go to him. But the most I've been upset about since the sixth grade has been bad grades. Sex and boys and life—haven't had to go there yet.

I take a deep breath. "I'm just having a hard time with my friends. With Justin, Peter, and Susan." I leave out Barbara.

"Well, you are all growing up and now you are—" His face gets little red. "You are all dating and serious now, right?"

"Yeah."

"Things are always bound to change, Madeline. The sooner you learn that, the better off you'll be, as you become an adult. Things change, and often times they get more difficult." He looks at me with the serious father face, furry eyebrows knitted together and jaw tense.

"Some change would be good," I whisper. "But some other change isn't so good."

My father seems to know exactly what I'm talking about. "Maybe what you're feeling is a little growing pains. Maybe you're the one changing. Maybe you're outgrowing them."

"But, what do I do? They've been my friends forever. I don't know where else to go."

"Then you're going to have to accept the differences. Or make new friends." He sits down at the kitchen table. "You have to understand that you cannot change people and that not everything can be under your control."

I don't say anything.

Dad gets up and kisses the top of my head. "I know it's tough being fifteen."

I turn and look outside again and Dad goes upstairs. A few minutes later the shower is running. I go back to my room.

After awhile Dad knocks on my door and, without opening it, he says, "Madeline, by the way, Bubbie called last night when you went to bed. I don't think your mother remembered to tell you."

Right.

"Okay."

Bubbie.

A few moments later, after I'm sure Dad is gone, I dial her number in California. I wish Bubbie had come to the wedding. But my *mother*—I know it wasn't Barbara who asked Bubbie not to come.

At the first ring, I'm seized with panic. What am I going to say? Justin and Barbara are drunks and I'm sick of pretending, Peter and Susan just had sex, and I feel totally alone? I know Bubbie. She'll listen and give great advice and call Dad to let him know the boy I'm seeing is drinking and his own daughter is too; I have never, ever seen Bubbie drink. Barbara says the one time she saw Bubbie drink was the last time she came for Rosh Hashanah. When I go visit her and we go out to dinner, she never even glances at the wine list. When we go to parties at her friends' houses, I have tried to sneak some champagne or wine. She always catches me and snatches the glass out of my hand. It's the only time I ever see her look angry.

I hang up the phone. I can't call her. I sit down on my bed and stare out the window. My tree's branches look like arms stretching out toward me. I wish I could run to them. I wonder if my father was right. Maybe I'm trying to control stuff I have no control over.

Tomorrow is Monday. School. Justin and Susan. And Peter. At least I have another week before Barbara returns from the honeymoon.

CHAPTER 9

I get to school early to avoid seeing everyone. My locker is all the way at the end of the corridor, far away from Justin and Peter's. I want to get my books and go to study hall early. I need to drop off a couple of depressing poems I wrote last night for the literary magazine. The deadline is today.

A pink notice hangs on the inside door of my locker as a reminder: "Lincoln High Dance Team: First meeting October 5. After School. All of last year's members must attend."

Susan and I are on the team together.

I could quit.

They'll never know.

I was just an alternate last year.

They probably don't even care.

Joanna Garin, senior captain of the dance team, breezes by. "I'm going to see you this afternoon, right? You're being nominated as the alternate to become a full member of the squad."

I smile feebly. "Yeah, I'll be there."

Great.

I drop off my poems on the way to study hall in the cafeteria. I won't see Peter or Susan until lunchtime. We don't have any classes near each other. And maybe Justin will be late for school so I won't have to see him in study hall. I'm not even sure where we stand right now. Did we break up? Should we?

At two o'clock I head for the dance team meeting, feeling victorious. I made it through the day without seeing any of them. Instead of walking the long way to English so I can pass Justin going to Biology, I take the short route through the library. Instead of meeting Peter and Susan after my Pottery class so we can walk together to the History hallway where we have class next door to each other, I sprint through the media center.

Unfortunately, lunchtime is here and my turkey and cheese sandwhich is screaming at me. In the cafeteria, Susan hurries up to me with this weird look on her face. "Oh, Madeline, God, I'm so sorry about Justin." She puts her hand on my arm.

I jerk away and say, irritated, "What? What about Justin?"

"You mean you don't know?" She is in drama mode.

"Susan, obviously I don't know."

"God, the police were called and everything-"

"Susan, what are you talking about?"

"Justin had some pot in his locker and—"

"What? When?"

"Second period. I guess he came in late and some teacher caught him in the hallway after passing time and smelled pot on him. Then they searched his locker. I was in Geometry, sitting by the door. I saw everything."

"They took him away?" I feel like a corpse.

"Yeah, and—"

I run out of cafeteria and through the heavy red doors to the outside.

I'm crying and running. I'm not surprised, but it confirms so much—that he's totally out of control and very, very far away from me. Where is he now? Did they lock him up? God, he's only fifteen!

I finally stop running at the top of the street to our neighborhood. I sit down on the side of the road, panting, clutching my history book and notebook. I don't know what to do.

I can't sleep that night. I lie in my bed with the window open. I feel a slight breeze, warm for this time of the year. I hear crickets and smell the remaining flowers from my mother's gardens. The corpse feeling has stayed with me. My eyes are opened so wide they hurt. What am I waiting for?

"Maddie? Maddie?"

The top of someone's head bobs up and down outside my window. Maybe I'm dead.

"Maddie, please come outside. Please." It's Justin.

I push myself up and lean against the screen to peer down at him. "Justin," I say, my nose against the screen. "What are you doing? Aren't you supposed to be in jail or something?"

"You heard about—"

"Yeah."

"Just come outside, please."

"Why? So we can fight over another stupid thing you've done?"

He looks away. "Please, I need to talk to you."

I try to take a deep breath, but I can't. I feel tight inside. "Okay."

I roll out of bed and slide into my blue slippers and robe and hurry soundlessly down the hall and to the back door. I open it quietly and step into the mudroom, then close the door to the rest of the house behind me. I slip out, leaving the mudroom door open, and scurry around to other side of the house. Justin is still standing under my bedroom window. The moon is high and bright, lighting up the yard. The low hum of crickets lets me know how late it really is.

He walks over to me right away and tries to hug me, but I'm stiff and motionless. A walking corpse. He pulls away. "Maddie, they didn't find anything in my locker. They just suspended me from school for a week and want me to see some drug counselor."

He continues to look at me, waiting for me to soothe him and tell him everything is okay and we'll all be fine. For the first time, I really don't feel like saying that. I keep my face and body rigid and stonelike. He comes closer and starts to kiss my face and whisper. "I love you, Maddie, please don't leave me. Please, give me another chance. I need you."

I continue to look past him, cold as a statue.

"Maddie—" He starts to kiss my mouth and push on my robe. I shove him away, really hard.

"Jesus, Maddie! Damnit!" He's trying not to yell. "What do you want from me? I'm not perfect. Is that it? I screw up—a lot. So what?"

I finally look at him. "I screw up too, Justin."

"Then what's the problem?"

"Are you going to see this counselor?"

He lets out a jagged, annoyed breath. "That's what this is all about? You know, Maddie, your sister drinks a lot. What's the big deal? She likes to have fun. I like to have fun. You never say anything to her, do you?"

I freeze again. We have never talked about Barbara's drinking. He knows nothing about what I feel or the new feelings or anything. No one knows. "You don't know anything about my sister," I snap back at him, "and it's really none of your business right now."

"Oh, that's a nice thing to say to your boyfriend."

"Before I can stop myself I say, "You're not my boyfriend.""

He ignores that. "This is about the other night. Drinking or no drinking, I still want to—you know, go further and stuff. I haven't changed, Maddie, I have just gotten to be fifteen. This is normal. I've grown up. You haven't—you and Susan and Peter." He says their names in this sarcastic, mocking tone.

"So, drinking and sex—that makes a grownup? This is the same bull you said the other night. You know what? I'd rather stay a kid forever."

We both look away. For a long ten seconds. The crickets crank up the volume.

"You know what, I'm tired of trying. You don't like me the way I am, then—well, let's just end this or whatever."

He didn't even hear me say that he wasn't my boyfriend. He is so out of touch.

We stare at each other, expressionless, like strangers on a subway.

Then I turn and walk away.

CHAPTER 10

"Did you actually break up?" Joanna Garin asks me. She picks up her dance bag; it's the end of practice. It is two weeks exactly since I met Justin under my window, two weeks exactly since I have spoken to him.

"Well, yeah. I said he wasn't my boyfriend any more, and he said, 'Lets end this,' so we did," I sound more calm and cool than I feel.

"Oh, my God," Joanna says. "You seem so okay and everything. If John and I broke up, I don't think I could even go to school and see him in the hallway."

"I don't know if I'm okay. I don't know what else to do except be really busy." The way I have been coping is to put up a big brave face during the day and cry myself to sleep at night while blasting "In Your Eyes" in my CD-man. In study hall I read my new self-help book *Good Women Who Love Bad Men.* It's incredible. *"The Bad Boy is the moody man who is sweet to you and rough to everyone else. He makes you feel special and wanted. If you ever start to challenge his Bad Boy behavior, he'll turn on you too…"* I should call Bubbie and tell her about it.

"Whatever you're doing, I wish I could be like that. John and I had a fight the other night about going to Homecoming. He doesn't want to go because he's in college now and thinks all this high school stuff is stupid. So I was, like, crying and begging. When we got off the phone, I felt so stupid. Why did I get so crazy over this? You know, why do I like this guy so much?" We walk out of the cafeteria together. She is giving me a ride home.

Exactly. Why do we like these jerks so much?

"So," she continues, "so, we are going to Homecoming but he refuses to go to dinner with all my friends, and he said that we have to go to his frat party after. He's such a jerk. But then again, he's also so hot and so sweet to me. He writes me all these letters about how he misses me. You know?"

"Yeah, I know. But maybe you have to get really sick of the way he treats you. You have to get so fed up, you decide you'd rather be alone than be with someone who makes you feel so bad." Another lesson from *Good Women Who Love Bad Men*. From the chapter "How to Move On."

Joanna unlocks the passenger's side of her silver Toyota Corolla. "I don't know, Maddie. You seem to have it all figured out. But I think I'm different from you. I'd rather be with someone and be treated like this than be alone. Isn't that pathetic?"

All I could think was, Yes, that is.

After The Night, as I think of it, I asked Joanna for another chance to try out for the dance team. Considering my Justin crisis the day of tryouts, she let me. I made it, and Susan is an alternate. We have very limited contact. The girls on the team have been especially nice to me. Not that they weren't before, but they all know what happened with Justin and the suspension.

I keep thinking about how I don't want to wind up like Joanna. I don't want to fall apart because some guy—even if it is Justin—doesn't treat me right. Even though it hurts so much not to be with him, when I'm with him lately I feel worse. What I want and miss is the old Justin, and I don't know where he is.

Besides avoiding Justin, Peter, and Susan and going to dance rehearsals, I've spent my time at literary magazine meetings. And guess what? The editor, a senior named Amy, is dating another member of the Jerk of the Month Club. She always asks my advice about what she should do with this guy, Ed. He won't talk to her in school, but they go out every weekend and have sex and drink. Ed has tattoos and a nose ring. He calls her slut and bitch and then tells her he's just kidding. Amy says her mother hates him, and all her friends tell her he's a loser, but she can't stay away from him.

"Amy, you're such a great person. I mean, you deserve so much better than some shithead guy who verbally abuses you!" It's the next afternoon, and I'm trying out some stuff from my new book. I just read the chapter called "Why Do I Love It When He Hurts Me So?" Amy and I are going through some magazine submissions. Everyone else is at the computer lab doing editing. "See, abuse does not just mean physical but also emotional and verbal." Like when Justin called me a bitch and made me feel bad for not let him go down my pants—verbal and emotional abuse. Amy knows nothing about what's gone on between Justin and me. She just knows we broke up.

"Where do you come up with this stuff? Am I really the senior and you're the sophomore?" Amy frowns. "I'm not a great person." She shuffles some papers around on the table. "I'm way too emotional and I just give my heart out to anyone walking by. I'm an idiot."

"No! Listen, you're nice and funny and a really great editor. Your only problem is low self-esteem."

Amy laughed. "How do you know so much?"

I pull out my book. "Go buy it!" I tell her.

So that's how things have been over the last couple of weeks. I keep thinking about how mad I am that the people who are supposed to be trying to help me feel better—my close friends—are way too distracted with themselves to even bother noticing how miserable I am. I know I have been avoiding them, and when Peter has called, I tell my parents I'm studying or about to shower or whatever. But doesn't Peter notice that or that I no longer talk to him or sit with them at lunch? And since the day I saw Susan after school and she told me about Justin, she hasn't said so much as hello to me.

And what about my parents? Haven't they noticed how depressed I am? I guess because I'm always at some meeting or rehearsal they just figure I'm tired and really busy. I know I'm not exactly free with my emotions. On top of all this, we have barely seen Barbara since they got back from the honeymoon.

So the way I have been dealing is to focus solely on school.

I cry myself to sleep every night, and the thing is, I'm crying over everything: Justin, Peter, Barbara, and even Susan. Even though I feel really tired, it's hard to go to sleep with all these thoughts. What if Barbara forgets about me? I mean I'm no longer useful to her. Plus, she seems happier away from the family and me. Maybe it's a cover up though. Maybe she's really miserable and Michael won't let her see me or talk to me. Then I get this panicky feeling. What if she wants to talk and she can't get to me? But we had dinner with the whole family at Chang's in Stamford the night they came back, and she didn't seem too interested in talking to me then.

All through the spring roll and steamed mushroom appetizers, Barbara went on and on about her new job at the hospital as a nurse's aid (Michael's idea) and their new apartment. "I'm even thinking about maybe going to school to become a nurse!" She didn't say as much as two words to me. Didn't ask anything about Justin or Peter. Nothing. I felt like dirt.

Michael was beaming too and talking about how they are making their second bedroom into a study for Barbara so when she starts classes she has a place to work. "We just bought her a new computer," he said, clasping her hand and kissing it.

All I kept thinking was, "Bullshit." I just know it is all temporary. My sister has never followed through with any of her career schemes. Plus, since when did she want to become a nurse? What happened to art?

I looked at Michael with total disdain because he and I had been close, and now he barely acknowledged my presence except to whisper, "Hey Mad, doesn't Barbara seem great? I told you everything would be fine."

That was about three weeks ago and I haven't seen her since. My parents seem more relaxed, and they don't sound worried when they mention her. I feel like getting a pan and hitting everyone over the head. Don't they realize that Barbara is a walking time bomb, and this whole getting married thing is a temporary distraction? I keep sensing that something is about to give, any minute. It's just a feeling.

It's the end of October and the dance team is getting ready for our first concert, so I have had a three-hour rehearsal almost every day. Susan and I ignore each other at rehearsal. Peter comes to get her after and he barely nods at me. I feel like even if we tried to hang out again, they wouldn't understand how I feel about Justin, and I would end up feeling more alone. But I miss them, a lot. After the concert, only my parents are in the lobby to greet me. Peter and Susan don't even glance my way, and my sister is working late at the hospital and can't come. I'm crushed. My friends are ignoring me, and Barbara has never missed a concert.

The following Friday is my mother's birthday. My sister, who can't even boil water, invites us over for dinner. She and Mom have been getting along great; they even went on a little shopping trip together last week. The happier everyone else seems, the more miserable I become. I feel invisible. My sister and I haven't done anything alone together since before the wedding. But for the birthday dinner, Barbara asks me to come over early and help. Michael is out of town for the weekend at some medical conference.

She's going to pick me up in a half-hour, and for the first time in a long while, I feel happy. I sit in the kitchen editing some of the short stories that have been submitted to the Literary Magazine. Each of us took home three stories for the weekend. Mensch has decided to fall asleep on a piece called "I Was a Teenage Alien." Maybe Mensch can conveniently go to the bathroom on it too, because I don't have the heart to tell Ginny, this skinny-as-a-stick ninth-grader with acne, that her story sucks. Anyway, as I'm correcting the words "a lot" (some one had smashed them together), the phone rings and since both of my parents are not home yet, I reach for it, hoping it's Peter or Justin or even Susan.

"Hello?"

"Um, uh—Madeline?"

I can't quite place the voice. "Yeah? Who's this?"

"Sean. Sean Dunay. Angie Dunay's younger brother?" He seemed to be asking me whether he was or not.

How weird! Well, maybe I need this right now. It's not as if I have anything else going on. I take a deep breath, pull my mouth away from the phone and let it out.

I go back to the phone. "Yeah, hi."

"I know this sounds kind of weird. But I've been wanting to call you, but I kept thinking you'd think I was some sort of freak or something. I mean I just asked for your phone number, like, two seconds after I saw you. But I never do anything like that, and—well, whatever. The reason why I'm calling is because my school is putting on a play version of *The Little Prince* and I'm in it. I play one of the guys the Little Prince visits. I play the tippler."

Isn't life just too ironic? "The guy who drinks all day." I half ask and half tell him. I have a strong feeling I need to go see this play. "Sure. When is it?"

"Tomorrow night."

"Great. Where should I meet you?"

"Come to Darien High at 6:30. I probably won't be able to see you before the show, but I'll see you after."

"Do you even remember what I look like?" I ask him.

"Yeah, you look like Madeline."

Feeling incredible because of my upcoming date and because my sister and I will have a couple hours alone, I practically skip to Barbara's '94 Accord when it pulls into the driveway.

"You look all happy," she says. "Want to tell me about it?"

But I'm too frozen to speak. I can smell alcohol on her breath.

Fifteen minutes later we arrive safely at her apartment, but I'm really thrown off because Barbara would never drink and drive. Anytime she's been drinking someone else has been driving. I'm also a little thrown off because I haven't seen her drink since the wedding. I haven't been around her much, but this just seems weird.

It wouldn't be normal to say, "Hey, are you drinking?" She doesn't know I think she has a problem. At least that's what I have always assumed. I feel confused and off balance.

We get out of the car and she grabs my hand. "Maddie, I have missed you so much! I've just been so busy with the new job and the apartment—and my new wifely duties." She says the last part with a sarcastic laugh.

"Yeah, I've missed you too. So much is going on now with everything."

"It's a good thing you and Justin broke up. You know, he's awfully young to be drinking so much." I had told her about the breakup in the car, but I hadn't mentioned the drinking. How did she know?

We go inside the large apartment-complex lobby, which is clean and simple with dried flowers and potpourri on the coffee table and a floral patterned couch.

"What do you mean?" I ask her.

She presses the third-floor button. "I used to hear you argue with him on the phone about the drinking and the leaving you alone at parties, the not showing up. I'm not completely self-absorbed, you know. I just never said anything because you never mentioned it to me." She says all of this lightly and casually. But it's a big deal to me. Where is this coming from?

"I wasn't really sure if I was making too big of a deal about it." Oh my God, I'm back to pretending again. What am I doing? This is a perfect opportunity to ask her about her drinking—and especially her drinking and coming to pick me up. I mean, she's not drunk, but it takes a lot to get my sister drunk. What I smell on her is beer. Okay, maybe she only had one.

Of course, I say nothing.

"Maddie, it's a big deal if it upset you. I always wondered why you didn't tell me about that. I'm not as clueless as you think. I know you worry about everything. You're the little worry wart in the family."

I'm unsure what to say next, but she pretty much takes care of that. "Michael told me about the Al-Anon meeting he dragged you to in the spring." She hands me her purse while she unlocks the door to her apartment.

Now I get it.

I follow her in, clutching the purse.

"I just want you to know," she says, "that I have it under control now. I know I was drinking like a total alcoholic before, but now I'm happier. I don't need to drink as much. I never realized how much I hated living at home until I left." She takes her purse and I follow her into the kitchen, where she puts her purse on the table and pours us each a glass of Dr. Pepper.

I'm still speechless. All I can manage is to stare at her and sip my soda.

"Sometimes," she says, taking a long drink from her glass, "sometimes I felt like I needed to be the screw up in the family. Like that's what was expected of me. You know, that way everyone would feel useful compared to me. After all, if you have a screw up, then everyone else feels better about themselves, because it could be worse, *you* could be the screw up."

I still say nothing. I'm shocked we are even having this conversation.

"You know, Maddie, I have to say when Michael first told me about the meeting and then about how worried you guys were and how you actually wanted to have an intervention—I have to admit, I was pretty pissed off. You and I have always been so close, and I just thought I should have been hearing all of this from you."

I finally find my voice. "When did he tell you?"

My heart is pounding and my throat is dry because for so long I have wanted everything to come out. But I thought I would have all the words planned. I'm caught so off guard.

"We got into a fight the second night of the honeymoon because I drank way too much. I was nervous, you know. It was starting to sink in that we had just gotten married. It was starting to feel real. So I'm all drunk and crazy and Michael has seen me like this before. Only now, as he said that night, 'You're my wife. Wives don't do this!' Isn't that funny—like boom! You're married and you're no longer who you've always been." She shakes her head and walks over to the sink and rinses her glass out.

She turns around, still holding her empty glass. "So it all came out, which is a good thing, because that stuff should really be out and talked about before you're married. He told me about the meeting you guys went to and how worried and scared you guys have been. Then, of course, he says how he thought getting married would change everything, and I just laughed in his face because that's Marriage 101: Don't expect to change anyone. So we went to bed and the next morning we sat, soberly, and hashed everything out between us, like our expectations and the things we were scared of and what we wanted in life."

I want to ask her where her drinking is at this point and what all this has to do with me.

She answers both questions before I can ask.

"I told him that I would try to drink less, and he agreed to be patient and not try to change me. We also talked about my whole job thing and he suggested the nurse's aid thing. I agreed to that because, honestly, Twist ain't cutting it, and I really don't know what I want." She is staring at me, and I know she's waiting for a reaction.

"Maddie, I have to say when we first got back, I really couldn't face you alone. I wasn't sure how to approach you about all this because you've never said anything. I was sad and mad, and well, now we're alone. So, do you have anything you need to say?"

The first thing that comes to my mind is, "Are you mad at me?"

"No! I felt more hurt than mad. You apparently think I'm a lush or something. You know, I started to wonder if Mom and Dad thought the same thing. But they've never said anything. Like you."

"You and Mom seem to be getting along better."

"That's because I'm decorating my apartment. We have something in common for once."

In the moment of silence, I start to simmer. Why am I worried if she's mad at me? She's got it all figured out. All my pent-up anger from the past few months starts to shift and move. I can't sit here and not say what I really feel. I just can't do it any more.

I take a deep breath, and then I tell her the truth. "Barbara, I've been thinking about the past a lot since the Al-Anon meeting, and looking back, I really am able to see all the messed up stuff you did and the position I was put into—being your, like, enabler." I have never said the word out loud and it sounds funny. But I keep going like a dam breaking loose. "You know, when I was ten, I was helping you sneak in the back door and getting you into bed and checking to make sure you were breathing. Then I was covering for you when you didn't get home on time, and even the day of your wedding, I was dragging you out of bed and getting you ready. Then you get married and you dump me." She looks pretty pissed off at this point, and her arms are tightly crossed but I don't care. I feel myself breaking free.

"And you know what? I'm sorry if you were hurt because I never told you how I felt, but to be honest with you, I never thought my feelings mattered because *poor Barbara.* Mom and Dad are so careful around you, and all the expectation is on me, and you have gotten away with living at home and not going to college and not ever having a real job. I know they would never put up with that from me, and also you partied and partied and no one has ever said a word to you. Ever. I say I'm going to a party and Mom and Dad give me a curfew of, like, nine. You never had one. So maybe you were the designated screw up, but it never seemed to bother you because you kept on screwing up!"

I walk over to her and put my cup in the sink. "By the way, what does 'cut back on drinking' mean, exactly? Does that include not tossing back a few before you pick up your little sister and bring her over to your house for some sisterly bonding?"

Now she is crying.

But I'm on a roll.

"How much did you drink before you came to pick me up?" I look over at the recycle bin and see at least six empty beer bottles. "Is it so awful to be around me that you have to get yourself drunk?"

She is hysterical now and not even looking at me.

I knew all along her story was an act. "Michael may buy this whole 'not drinking as much' thing, but I know you better." I stare at her for a few moments. Then I storm out the door.

I convince my mother I'm really sick, and they should go without me to dinner at Barbara's. It's not a lie, because when I finally reached home after about an hour of walking and then a ten-minute bus ride, I threw up. When my parents came home I was lying on the couch in the basement. I physically felt fine but I was a mess inside.

What have I done? Now that it is all out, what do I do?

In my bedroom, I stare out the window at the leaves on the oak tree. They've begun to change to brilliant yellows, oranges, and reds. I'm crying. I wish I could call Peter. I wish I could call Bubbie. I wish I could do something to relieve the heartache.

But never once do I regret telling Barbara the truth.

CHAPTER 11

"Why do you need a ride to Darien High School?" In my parents' huge bedroom, my mother is grilling me for information about the play tonight. She is ensconced in her little workstation: sewing machine, desk, and a mountain of extra material of the floral persuasion.

"Why aren't you going with Peter or Justin?" Her reading glasses slide down to the end of her nose. She glances briefly at me then goes back to hemming my sister's drapes, her brow furrowed in concentration. Then she stops and puts her hand to my forehead. "Do you feel well enough to go out?"

The dinner at Barbara's was "delicious," and my parents were shocked at their daughter's "domestic bliss," as my mother referred to it. I guess Barbara cleaned herself up before everyone arrived yesterday. At first I felt really sad, but today I'm just pissed off. She asked me how I felt. She accused me of not telling her my feelings, and so I told her, and now she probably hates me. I wonder if she and I will ever discuss what happened.

I don't hate myself though. Maybe a few months ago I would have. But I believe that considering I really didn't have time to think about what I should say or how I should say it, I said the things that I needed to.

I'm trying to push all of that aside tonight. I need a night away from everything. I'm sort of looking forward to the play, even though it will probably depress the hell out of me.

"Mom, I'm just going to a play, not some raging party. What's the big deal?"

"While I'm delighted"—she pauses to stick another pin in the hem—"that you are not going to some raging party, I'm also concerned because you usually do everything with Peter, Susan, and Justin. What's going on?"

Hey, I guess she has noticed something.

"I'm just trying to hang out with different people. Make new friends." I really don't want to get into the whole not-talking-to-my-friends thing.

She stops playing with the hem and takes her glasses off. "I think I know what's going on."

Huh?

"You miss your sister."

What?

"I know that the two of you were very close. And you haven't been the same since she moved out."

Now I try not to become visibly unhinged.

"Listen, I know that she shared many things with you, and in many ways, you were her big sister. I know at times I got on her case, and you defended her or you tried to make her feel better. This must be hard for you, to—in a sense—lose her."

Part of me wants to tell my mother everything that has been going on and how agonized I have been. But I don't know where to start, and I'm scared of her reaction. Do I tell her all about the drinking? Will she believe me? I don't tell her anything, but I also don't actually deny that things aren't okay.

"Mom, I'm fine. I just need to go out tonight, okay?"

"Barbara told me the two of you had a little argument yesterday and that you left her apartment and ran all the way home."

I look down at my nails and pick a cuticle.

"She didn't tell me what it was about. But she didn't have to. I know that you miss her and that you wish she would spend more time with you." My mother pulls my hand away to stop the cuticle picking. "Honey, she has her own life now, and she'll be starting her own family. Believe me, this is a good thing for her. She needs this."

I know the tears are leaking out of my eyes. All I can think about is this stupid time when Barbara came in through the back door at three in the morning when I had a little sleepover and we were all still up. She walked in without a shirt on, in just her bra. She had gotten a small tattoo of a rose on her shoulder and for some reason she thought it was very funny, and it hurt so much she had to keep her shirt off. She came inside cracking up. The image of her laughing and holding her shirt and the faces of my friends makes me want to both laugh and cry.

"Maddie?"

I wipe my eyes. I hate crying in front of Mom because it seems pointless to her.

She sits with her hands in her lap, watching me.

So I say, "I just want to go to this play tonight. Can you drive me?"

"Okay," she says softly. She doesn't even admonish me as I wipe my nose with the back of my hand. She just passes me a couple of tissues. At least I didn't get my snot on any draperies or furniture.

❧   ❧   ❧

"What are you doing there?" the little prince says.
"I'm drinking," the tippler/Sean replies.
"Why are you drinking?" the little prince asks.
"So that I may forget," the tippler/Sean answers.

He says this with such creepy realism that I want to run out of the cafetorium. Luckily, I find a napkin in the bottom of my purse, because the moment the play began, I felt my eyes fill up. In the first act, the little prince tells the story of how he had to leave his beloved flower behind on his home planet because "I was too young to know how to love her." Ever since, the little prince, desperate to leave his love behind and forget about her, has traveled all over the galaxy. Now he is on the planet with the "drunk."

"Forget what?" the little prince asked.
"Forget that I'm ashamed."
"Ashamed of what?"
"Of drinking."

Although I'm supposed to be going out to escape my problems and made a solemn promise to myself not to think about Barbara or Justin, now I feel like I wasn't supposed to do that. Every scene has a message just for me. During this tippler scene, all I'm thinking is that Justin only drinks to forget about his dad and to forget about when his life felt more normal. But now he's been drinking so much, it's as if he forgot that he began to drink because of his dad. Now he's in this cycle. He drinks not just to forget his dad, but also to forget the shame he feels about drinking. My heart aches for him and for the reality that I can't help him. And my sister—that's a whole lot worse and a whole lot more complicated. She seems to have herself and probably Michael convinced that she isn't drinking *as much* and that this is okay. I feel hopeless about Barbara. I can't reach her, because she has already made up her mind.

When the play ends, I'm not sure if I want to go see Sean. I feel like this date—if that's what it's supposed to be—shouldn't happen. I'm way too sad. I loiter on my way to the lobby. I will congratulate Sean and then call my mother to come get me, even though I told her I would get a ride home.

I see Sean immediately: not too tall, with a bigger build than Justin's, a relaxed looking smile, and dark brown eyes. He waves me over as if I'm an old friend.

"Hey!"

I'm not sure how to greet him. "You were really good," I say awkwardly.

"You liked the show?" He smiles again. "You know, I wasn't even sure if I should have called you—"

"No! I'm really glad I came—"

"I just thought you'd really appreciate this."

In more ways than one. Suddenly I remember him reading the book at Barbara's wedding. "So that's why—"

"I was reading the book, yeah. I had never read it before, and I figured I'd better read about the tippler at least. But I wound up liking the book and reading the whole thing a couple times."

A petite brunette runs up to Sean and hugs him. "You were so great! I'm so proud of you!"

"Thanks. Angie, this is Madeline."

She grabs my hand and says, "Little Maddie! Not so little any more!"

She kisses Sean's cheek and gives me a little wave as she leaves.

We share an awkward pause, and I realize I need to cut this short.

"I really enjoyed the play," I say with more awkwardness than I would have thought possible.

"Want to come to the cast party?"

"I really have to get home."

He looks disappointed. "Okay, how about a ride?"

In the car Sean turns on the radio. K-Rock is playing twenty-four hours of Led. My father introduced me and my friends to Led Zeppelin when we were kids. When my mother was out of the house, he blasted "The Ocean" and "Ramble On" while we played air guitar and jumped around like crazed hippies from the seventies. Justin and I played Led Zeppelin after school, background music at first for doing homework and later for making out. Now the music is one more sign of the past, like a final goodbye.

"So you liked the play?" Sean asks.

"Huh? Yeah, it was cool." How obvious is it I'm on another planet?

A moment of silence. Then Sean pulls over to the side of the road. "Madeline?" He looks down at his hands and speaks to the steering wheel.

"Yeah?" I'm still far away.

"I know that I only know you from when we were little, and it's not like I'm expecting anything from you. But you seem like you don't want to be here. You seem like you didn't really want to go out with me tonight." He is still talking to the steering wheel.

"Well, I…uh…" I can't think of anything to say. I'm so tired. I just want to go home, have a nice cry, wake up, and start over. I steal a glance at Sean, to see if he's completely pissed off.

He catches my eye. "You know, you seem sort of sad. But I don't think you're a sad person. You're just sad right now." The faint, spicy scent of Sean's aftershave floats between us, and I think, yeah…I am. So. Sad. And so tired of feeling alone. The bass chords of Led Zeppelin drum in my ears, and the combination of music and melancholy makes me dizzy. We look into each other's eyes a moment too long. Sean's eyes aren't just brown, but warm, Hershey's Kiss brown. Chocolate, liquid. I yearn for some comfort for my loneliness.

Without planning to, I lean toward Sean as he leans toward me, and we kiss gently. I pull him toward me more and we kiss with more intensity. As soon as warmth spreads over me, I start to see Sean as the tippler and remember how sad I feel. It's as if I have to finish feeling the sadness before I can move on to feeling good. As if I have to let all the sadness out.

I stop kissing Sean and slowly pull away. Tears stream down my face. I don't bother rubbing my eyes or straightening my clothes. I don't want to stop this gush of feeling.

Sean doesn't say anything. He pulls me back to him, not to kiss me but just to hold me and stroke my head. I bawl like a baby. We sit this way for a while, and eventually the tightness in my body drains away, leaving me warm and exhausted.

Still, Sean stays silent. It's as if he accepts that this girl he took out is having a total breakdown and that's okay. It's just life. Wow. What a cool person.

I pull away and smooth my hair and use the back of my hand to wipe my face. Sean rummages around, finds a Dunkin' Donuts napkin, and gently wipes my eyes. He doesn't give me the napkin—which would have been sweet enough—but he *wipes my eyes.* Unreal.

I break the silence. "Thanks." Sean just smiles and continues to pat away my tears.

"Whoever he is, he did a number on you," he says, as he tucks the napkin into his cup holder.

"What do you mean?"

"Someone broke your heart. Some guy, probably. Right?"

I nod, then shake my head no. "It's not just about him. It's like recently my whole life has been…it's like everything in my life is not really the way I thought it was. Like some Twilight Zone episode."

"Suddenly?"

"No…gradually. I just took awhile to really 'tune in,' if you know what I mean."

He nods. "Yep, I know. Been there."

But he doesn't launch into his own sob story. He stays focused on me. He seems too perfect to be real.

"Sean, you're a pretty incredible guy. First I kiss you like a maniac, and then I cry like a five-year-old. And you take it all in like it's a normal way for a girl to be on a date." Even though I feel too tired to laugh, I manage a few chuckles.

"What do you mean? Most girls cry after they kiss me."

We both laugh weakly.

"Well…." I'm not sure what to do next. I just want to go home and rest. Sleep for a long time.

Sean is so awesome that he knows this before I say it. "Listen, I'll take you home. We can go out another time. You probably just need to sleep. It's seems to me like you were holding that in for awhile."

I lean over and kiss Sean on the cheek. "Thank you."

❧   ❧   ❧

I walk into the house around nine o'clock. Except for the front hall light, the house is dark. I walk into the kitchen and flick the light switch.

"Peter!" I shriek.

"Hi." He is at the kitchen table with a plate of sugar cookies and a glass of milk. My mother's work.

"What are you doing here?"

"I came by about an hour ago, and your mom said you'd be home by 9:30." He checks his watch. "You're early. Where'd you go?"

"I went to a play," I stammer out. "To see a friend in a play." Part of me wants to hug him hard and tell him what I just experienced. The other part of me is furious. How can he show up here and act like everything is normal?

"Who'd you go see? Someone from school?" He pushes his glasses up.

That ignites the fire in me. Despite my exhaustion, I muster up some steam.

"You know what, Peter? I'm not interested in making small talk with you. You don't talk to me for weeks and now you want to chat. Forget it." I open the fridge and take out a gallon of water. The water will help me wake up.

"Hey! Wait a minute." He stands up, snatches off his glasses, and glares at me. "You stopped talking to me, Maddie. I tried to talk to you. I was calling you all the time and leaving messages. I finally stopped because you never called me back."

I slap the plastic bottle of water onto the counter. "What do you want?"

He moves across the kitchen and grabs my hands. "Maddie, what's going on? Why have you been avoiding me?"

I want to let everything out. But I feel hurt, still, and I'm also not ready yet to deal with him. I pull my hands away.

"Maddie? What's happening?"

"I don't know what to say to you," I whisper.

"What do you mean?"

"I feel so far away and so out of your life. I feel like so many things have changed, and I don't know where I fit in." I get a glass from the cabinet in front of me.

"Because of Susan and I—because we—she told you, right?" He sighs. "I really wish I had been the one to tell you. I felt weird about you and her discussing—"

"There was no discussion. Susan sort of burst out with it." I pour a glass of water so I don't have to look at him. "It just was sort of at the wrong time—when she told me."

"Yeah, she has a habit of that."

I take a long drink.

"So, what's happening with Justin?" Peter asks.

"It's over."

"Good. He's been a real ass for a long time now. It's good to know you're done with him."

Somehow Peter's mini speech doesn't make me feel any better.

"Listen," he says. "I have to know this. Were you mad at me because I slept with Susan? Because I'm happy and you're not?" He puts his glasses back on as if he needs them to see my answer.

"What?"

"Well, Susan says—"

I cut him off. "That's it. That's exactly what I need from you. Thanks for your support. If this is why you came over here, goodbye." I slam the glass down and head for the stairs.

"Madeline?" Mother calls. "Are you home? Peter's here for you."

"No, he's not," I whisper and stare at him.

Peter grabs his brown suede coat that is resting on the coat hook beside the pantry. As he strides out the front door, I realize that I have officially lost everything.

CHAPTER 12

I'm too exhausted to sleep. Instead, I stay awake until 3 o'clock thinking. Peter is gone. Justin is gone. Susan—that bitch. Telling Peter I'm pissed because they are happy? What the hell is that? Can either one of them think about anyone but themselves? I think about Sean. That makes me smile, but then I feel scared. I don't want to start another relationship. I don't want any more heartache for a while.

I fall asleep for a few hours and wake up around eight. My mother is gone when I get up, and my father is on his way out to an all-day conference on this new instrument that measures ocean waves or something. His research department invented it. I decide it's time to call Bubbie.

She answers on the second ring.

"Maddie!"

The sound of her voice is so comforting and stable that for the first time in several months I feel hope.

"Where have you been? You haven't returned any phone calls, and you're due for a visit very shortly," Bubbie says.

"Christmas vacation isn't for over two months, Bubbie."

"Well, we have lots to catch up on before you get here! If we wait until you're here, we'll have even more."

"I've been so busy…" I begin.

"Let's start with the wedding. How was it?"

We discuss the wedding for a few minutes I tell her about the blue nightmare dress. Dancing with all the old guys. The floral napkins and tablecloths. But Bubbie is no idiot. She can tell when I'm upset.

"What's wrong, Maddie?"

I hesitate. How much should I tell her? Will she tell my father?

"I'm having some problems with my friends."

"Good old Peter and Susan? What about Justin, the love of your life?"

She asks about my friends as if she knows them, and she hasn't seen them since they were little kids. She's such a cool grandmother.

In a rush I tell her everything except how Justin pressured me about sex—that was too embarrassing—and Sean and the kiss. I also conveniently leave out the whole Barbara thing.

There's a long silence. I listen to Bubbie's deep breathing. "I think this is partly my fault," she tells me.

What?

"Honey, there's something I want to tell you about myself and your mother."

What does this have to do with what's happening to me?

"Listen to me carefully. I know what Justin is doing. I used to do it."

"Do what?" I ask stupidly.

"Drink."

Silence.

"Madeline?"

She speaks as if the words were apples, and she's looking for the un-bruised ones. "You're right, he is very sad and in a lot of emotional pain and that's why he's drinking. But he's also being very selfish and mean to you and probably his mother. That's what alcohol does to people."

I don't want to hear what she's telling me. I want to hang up the phone. I feel like I'm watching a car accident about to happen, and I can't do anything except hide my eyes.

But I'm frozen to the phone.

"Maddie, I was in a lot of pain when your grandpa Charlie had cancer and all those years he was sick. When he died I drank like a fish. I lashed out at people I cared for, like Justin has done to you and Peter."

I can't picture it. I don't want to. "You could never be as nasty as Justin is," I choke out. I shove some of Justin's old love letters off my bed, sit at the edge, and grip the phone.

"One time—" Her voice catches. "One time, you were about nine or ten, the last Rosh Hashanah we had together. Well, I had brought wine to the dinner. But I had promised your mother I wouldn't drink. She got very upset with me and said some really mean things. I had already been drinking before I arrived, and she smelled it on my breath. She told me to leave. I was so out of control. I smacked her across the face when she told me she never wanted to see me again. That was the last time I saw her."

Oh my God! That's why Bubbie never drinks. That's why my mother is a total control freak. Oh, my God. My poor mother. We actually do have a lot in common. I don't know what to say to Bubbie. My hero, my perfect Bubbie.

"Now, I know you. Don't go doing this pedestal thing. I'm not perfect. I was wrong and awful and I'm very ashamed. But it's over, and I'm a faithful AA member." She sighs. "Look, I'm telling you that Justin needs help and not from you. You need to let Justin's mother and family deal with this."

Should I ask her about Barbara? "So is alcoholism hereditary?"

"It can be." She seems to be measuring her words. "If you believe, as I do, that we have a gene that predisposes people to have a problem with alcohol, then yes, it can be. Why do you ask? Have you been drinking?"

"No, but—" I stop myself. If I say this out loud to Bubbie, there's no going back.

"But what, sweetie?" she asks softly.

I start to cry because I know she already knows.

"Honey, now stay with me here." Bubbie's voice is like the finish line at the end of the race. I haven't made it yet, but I can see it's up ahead. "Tell me. What is it?"

"Barbara—" I can't get the words out. I just cry and cry.

"I know, I know."

I'm bawling now. "She—she—" I try to breathe "She drinks and she's trying to convince herself—Michael and me—that it's under control. Oh, Bubbie…. She's been drinking for years and no one—Mom and Dad—no one ever says anything. What's wrong with all of us? Why haven't we ever said anything, Bubbie? Why?"

"I have, sweetie. I have."

"You have?"

"Yes. And that's probably why your sister has stopped coming to see me," Bubbie tells me.

"When? When did you say something?"

"It was about two years ago when she was out for a visit. You weren't with her. She and I went out to dinner and she finally had her I.D. and wanted to order some drinks—"

"Where was I? Why wasn't I there?" I need to know. Somehow I would feel less anxiety right now if I could remember why I wasn't there.

"Let me see…I don't quite—oh, wait. You had the flu really bad. Remember?"

Now it mattered less. The flu. So what. "Oh, yeah. Anyway, what happened?"

"Well, she had quite a few. I knew immediately that she had a problem because it took about seven drinks to get her drunk. She must've been drinking for some time, with that kind of tolerance."

Bubbie didn't know the half of it.

She continues. "So I took her home, knew I couldn't talk to her until she had sobered up. The next morning I told her we were going to go meet some friends for brunch. I took her to an AA meeting instead. She said nothing to me at the meeting, and the only thing she said in the car was that she was booking an early flight back home. We didn't fight about it. We didn't talk about it." Bubbie pauses.

"I don't know what to say," I tell her.

"And you know, Maddie, Barbara is not stupid. She knew I had a drinking problem, and she knew it ruined my relationship with your mother. She knew because she was there when your mom and I had our fight. And I felt partly to blame because Barbara and I never talked about it. You know how careful we all are with her. We always have been, ever since she was born. We felt so sad for her that her father had abandoned her."

I feel a flicker of anger at all that being careful.

Bubbie sounds a bit angry too. "And I know how your mother is about not dealing with things. She'd rather brush it under the carpet or avoid it. That's why she doesn't talk to me."

"Do you think she knows Barbara drinks?"

"Oh, yes. She saw me drink. She knows the signs. But she probably feels guilty with Barbara and probably responsible. Both of your parents do." She sighs. "Some people feel that if you don't say it out loud, it doesn't exist. I called your father after that last visit, and even he didn't want me to get involved. Your dad's a pretty open guy, but he has his own guilt."

This is a lot for me to take in. I want to just hang up and sit with everything.

Bubbie blows her nose. "Barbara's not ready to talk to me. She didn't invite me to the wedding. She recommended that I don't come because of your mom. But I also know she didn't want me there."

I don't say anything.

"Oh, sweetie, you must be so overwhelmed. Do you want to call me back later? Maybe take some time to digest all this?"

I barely get out a yes before I hang up and curl up on my bed. I don't cry. I just stare at the only painting on my white walls Degas' *The Dance Class*, a gift from Mom. I feel an urge to reach out and touch it, like it might connect me to her. I have so many questions. I want to sit down with Bubbie and figure it all out or something. Why do people drink? Why did you drink? Maybe Bubbie can explain the thing I cannot understand about Justin and Barbara. A half hour passes and I dial Bubbie's number again.

She answers my questions with one of her own. "Why do human beings do any of these terrible, self-destructive things? I think it's about getting away from deep pain. Until I sobered up, I couldn't see how my drinking destroyed my relationships, my family, myself."

"But what can I do? I want to help. I don't get it. I tried to get Justin to talk—"

"Sweetie, this is a problem too big for you. And the truth is, no one can help an alcoholic until they're ready. Stop trying to fix Justin and Barbara. Work on yourself. You're very young. Learn now that people are full of things you can't fix."

I can't help Justin? But what about my family?

"So I guess I can't confront Mom and Barbara about all this? I guess I can't really do much, if they don't want to deal with it?"

"Honey, you can deal with it yourself. Why don't you start going to Al-Anon?"

I laugh. "Michael and I went in the spring. But now he thinks marriage will fix Barbara."

"Is that what he told you?"

"Yes."

She sighs again. "Maddie, I love you and think you're a really special young woman. My advice is to continue to be as sensitive and introspective as you are. Sweetie, you're terrific at self-examination. Continue that. Work on you."

After we get off the phone, I tear up all my love poems to Justin. I put the wedding picture of Barbara and me in my top dresser drawer. She was bombed out of her mind in that picture.

I sit for a long time looking out the window. The wind is gusty and sweeps the golden leaves off my tree, and even though the leaves were what made it so beautiful to me before, the bumps of the long, thick, bare branches strike me as breathtaking.

CHAPTER 13

✵

Barbara is sitting in her car in the driveway when my parents and I come home from dinner at Felix's restaurant. My insides freeze. She never just shows up. Maybe Michael is working another late shift at the hospital.

As we get out of the car, she walks over to us. "Hi guys!" Big smile. "Michael's got an overnight, and I was starting to get a little lonely at the apartment, so I thought I'd come home and spend a night in my old room."

Barbara knows my mother has turned her room into a guest bedroom. The once red and black walls are now light mauve. Mom replaced the black, pressboard furniture. Barbara bought it from Wal-Mart after a fight with Mom, during which she screamed, "It's my room! I'm sick of that stupid canopy bed. I hate that ugly oak dresser." Mom finally gave in when Barbara threatened to carve her name into all the furniture. Now the room has a white bedroom set covered with little hand-stenciled roses.

Now my mother, in her usual weekend uniform—pressed jeans and a navy sweater thrown over her shoulders—wipes an imaginary stain from her left thigh. She purses her lips and tugs at her sweater. She had been laughing and relaxed at dinner, telling us about how Mrs. Tilton, whose husband owns the Saxon Country Club, made my mother and her installer rehang the draperies for their living room four times.

"She just didn't like this crease or that fold or something inane like that. What a nut! Then she started to tell me about her high school drop-out daughter and her nose-pierced boyfriend." My mother had sighed in a total non—Martha Stewart way. I had actually enjoyed her conversation.

"Well, it's nice to see you Barbara." She looks from Barbara to me to my father. "Let's all go inside and I'll make us some vanilla almond tea."

My father, who had been knee-deep in his steak and French fries at dinner, laughing at Mom's story and holding her hand with his free one, now shifts from one leg to the other nervously. He rubs his hands together and says, "That sounds great. How about we all watch a movie tonight?" He forces a smile, looking from my mom to Barbara like a nervous puppy that wants to make his owners happy. "*Ishtar* is on at eight on HBO." My father loves Dustin Hoffman. Only this is a film even Dustin wants to forget.

"Stan, that's the worst movie," Mom says as we all walk through the breeze-way door into the mudroom.

"So Mom finally let you get the satellite TV?" My sister oozes sarcasm. "But she won't let you watch what you want."

My mother stiffens and I worry that pursing her lips so tightly will give her a cramp. "It won the worst award of 1987," I chime in. "I bet you like *Wag the Dog*, too, Dad."

"That was a great movie!" My father squeezes the back of my neck before we all shrug off our coats and, one by one, hang them up. It reminds me of kindergarten where we would all file into the classroom closet and wait our turns to hang our coats on the little wooden pegs.

We file in silence into the kitchen, and Mom fills the tea kettle, Dad gets four pink-and-green floral-patterned mugs from the cabinet, and I head for the pantry to get some Milano cookies—Mom's favorite.

Dad drops a teabag in each mug and says, "Lets make popcorn too." He looks at Barbara who is standing awkwardly next to the island in the middle of the kitchen. "Why don't you get out the old air popper?"

"I don't live here any more. I don't even know where you guys keep it." My sister's face looks like she's eating lemons. I bet she's pissed that she didn't get a rise out of Mom with her snotty comment. That we all didn't jump for joy when we saw her in the driveway.

Fifteen silent minutes later we are seated around the flat-screen TV in the family room. My father has the remote and we are looking at the TV guide menu on the screen.

"How about that freaky Stephen King movie, *Carrie*?" It's the first thing Barbara has said since the kitchen.

My mother shakes her head. "I'm not watching that horrible film."

"Hey, here's a favorite of your mother's." Dad clicks on a movie called *All About Eve*. Ironically, one of Bubbie's favorites too.

"That movie is a hundred years old!" my sister protests.

Here we go. My mother's face stiffens into the familiar look she gets whenever Barbara does something bratty.

I stay quiet and watch the drama unroll. Is my mother going to give in? Will Barbara stamp her feet, ball her fists, and scream, "WAAAAA!" Will Dad ever get to watch what he wants?

"What do you want to see besides *Carrie*?" my father asks patiently.

Barbara sulks. "I don't care. I don't live here anymore."

That's it. My mother has had it. Her face is bright red. "You're damn right you don't!" And she storms off to her and Dad's blue-and-white bedroom with chartreuse accents.

My sister looks over at me and laughs. Does she think Friday didn't happen? Six months ago I would have smiled and rolled my eyes and enjoyed this. But it's not six months ago. I don't smile. Don't roll my eyes. I get up and say, "I'm going to bed."

I can't believe what happens next. Just as I'm about to leave, my father gets up and without a word, follows my mother. Before Barbara got married, he would have stayed out here with us to watch the movie.

Maybe things have changed.

Maybe they know more than I realize.

My eyes fly open around two o'clock. I have to pee. As I stumble into the bathroom, I hear a sigh and the tinkle of glass. When I leave the bathroom, I hear it again. I freeze and listen. Again, the noise. All the rooms on this floor open into each other and we have cathedral ceilings, so you can hear everything. I follow the noise into the hallway, then through the living room, dining room, kitchen.

In the tiny library off the kitchen, Barbara is smoking a cigarette and drinking a beer. She is sitting on the couch, the window next to her open, with a *Vogue* in her lap.

What the hell is this? From the doorway of the TV room, I watch smoke form spirals around Barbara, making her look ethereal.

I feel annoyed, angry, and confused. "Barbara?" I whisper.

She turns, the haze of smoke settling, and stubs the cigarette out on the top of the bottle of Rolling Rock, then drops it into the opening. The light reflects in the window and on two empty bottles and a pack of Marlboro Lights. I grope for something to say into the thick air. Barbara's eyes are red, her hair matted to her head.

"Barbara, what are you doing?"

She gives the weirdest laugh. "What does it look like? Isn't this what you expect? Isn't this what you all expect from poor Barbara?"

She tosses the can on the floor. "Listen, Maddie, you're the ace in the family and I'm the fuckup. I'm sitting here awaiting my doom."

This drama is the last straw. I have had it with Barbara, and I don't care if I wake up the whole damned house. They can come and see her down here drinking and being the bum she is.

"No, you listen to me. You are not going to sit here and pull this shit in our house. Mom was right. You don't live here anymore. I don't even know why you came here tonight. And I'm sorry you're all messed up and you feel whatever—rejected or alone or separate or whatever. But you can't drag us down any more. Mom and Dad and I have let everything go, excused it away, but it hasn't helped you one damn bit. You want to destroy yourself? Do it alone." I feel like Wonder Woman. Like it's us against her.

"I've already destroyed myself, Maddie." She says pathetically.

"What happened to getting your drinking under control? What happened to the deal you made with Michael?"

"He's basically gone every other weekend. Working. Conferences. It's hard to be alone."

Her whiny voice makes me want to shake her. "What do you think I have been going through since you moved out? I have no friends and no sister." I stop for a moment, realizing that we both feel lonely. "Barb, I'm lonely too. I wish you could see—" I stop again, remembering Bubbie's advice: To deal with myself and stop trying to change Barbara.

"I thought you were glad I was gone." She pushes her hair out of her face. "You don't have to take care of me anymore."

I look at the beer bottles and Barbara's mournful face and feel like I have hit a wall. I'm not a superhero. I can't even deal with my own problems.

"I'm pregnant," Barbara bursts out.

The wall collapses and I sit down beside her. She grabs my shoulders and weeps in my arms.

That's why she came home.

CHAPTER 14

In the kitchen the next morning, I wonder if the night before was a dream. My mother is already up frying eggs, her face freshly scrubbed but tired looking. A pile of wheat toast waits on the golden oak kitchen table, already set with four peach-and-teal breakfast plates. "Eggs?" she asks.

"Sure." I grab some toast, butter it up, and sit down.

My father comes in, rubbing his eyes and yawning. His hair is sticking up and he's dressed in a rumpled dark green button-down shirt and pressed khakis. He has a talk to give this morning at the university. Apparently Mom got hold of the khakis but not the rest of him. "How nice of you to make breakfast!" He touches Mom's shoulder.

She squeezes his hand. Then her eyes scan his hair and pants. "Hon, I can iron your shirt, and there's a brush in the top drawer of the vanity in the bathroom down here." She doesn't sound like Martha when she talks to Dad. She sounds like when one of my friends tells me I have lettuce in my teeth—like she's just looking out for him, not ordering him to do something. But I picture her yanking Dad's shirt off, pulling out the portable ironing board she has in the hall closet—for emergencies—and pressing the shirt with the spare iron she has in the kitchen, under the sink. I can see her pulling a brush out of mid-air and taming his bird's nest hair.

He looks down at his shirt. "Don't have time. Plus all the mad scientists will look like this. I'll fit right in. How about I finish making the eggs and you sit down?"

My father is the only one who can soothe Mom's compulsion to iron the world flat. She sits next to me and pours orange juice for each of us. "Is Barbara still here?" Her voice is as flat as she wishes she could make Dad's pants.

"Yeah, she's probably still sleeping." I wonder if we remembered to put her beer bottles in the trash last night.

Barbara walks in, her hair wet and her jeans and sweater on, her shoes in her hand. "Mom, I'm sorry about being such a brat last night."

My mother puts down her juice glass, her face softening. "Why don't you stay for breakfast?"

Barbara and I exchange a look of silent understanding. Barbara can't stay because of her promise to me last night. After I told her about my phone call with Bubbie, Barbara swore she would go home first thing this morning and call her. Just before we went to bed, she told me, "I'm not saying that I'm ready for AA or anything, Maddie. I just know that this is really bad."

That had been enough for me.

"Thanks, but I have to get home," Barbara tells my parents now. "Michael will be back soon."

After she leaves, I think about the bombshell she dropped last night. You can't drink when you're pregnant. She told me the pregnancy was an accident. "This isn't in Michael's plan. I can't have this baby." I had asked her if she had told him. She said no. "You need to tell him," I said. "You don't know how he'll react. Besides, what will you do? Just have an abortion without telling him?" She didn't say anything. "Were you too drunk to remember to use protection?"

I finally asked Barbara something I have wanted to understand for a long time. Why does she drink so much? And she told me kind of what the tippler says in *The Little Prince*: "To escape the pain of living, of all my failures," she said. "Then you just keep drinking because you don't know what else to do."

I'm dying to tell my mother everything and to call Bubbie myself. That's what the old me might do. But I can't do this for Barbara. She has to do it herself.

❦   ❦   ❦

As I walk to my locker, I see Susan walking to hers. As I have every morning for the past month, I start to look away, but today I'm not quick enough and we make eye contact. She looks at me sadly. I flip open my biology book and pretend to check for my homework. When I reach in my locker to get my bag, I see a familiar pair of Nikes approaching and my heart skips. I haven't spoken to Justin in over a month. I haven't even seen him.

Justin reaches to help me get the bag and I snatch it away. His locker is on the other side of the building. He's here for a reason.

"Haven't seen you in awhile," he says.

"Well, I've been in school. Where have you been?"

"Here…sometimes."

The awkwardness rises between us like steam from boiling water. I shift my bag over my shoulder. With a surge of bravery, I look him in the face. "What do you want?"

"I already told you, and we both know I'm not going to get that." His hand moves toward me as if to grab my left breast. I can smell marijuana. I'm so tired of his crap. I feel my fist curl up, and before I know it, I drop my bag and clock him across the cheek.

"Oh my God!" Susan's voice rings out behind me.

Justin puts his hand to his blood-red face. He's so high; I don't even think he feels it. He starts to laugh. "You stupid bitch." Still laughing, he backs away.

I slam my locker shut, grab my bag and run until I'm out of the building and far from school.

Near Justin's street, I slow down to wipe away the tears and snot. This taking off from school is becoming a bad habit. When will I get caught?

I can't believe I actually hit Justin, even if he deserved it. I can't believe he is such a complete asshole. I can't believe how bad everything has gotten. And I can't believe I'm about to knock on his door.

When I knock, I can hear Casey scratch his way down the hall to the door.

"Casey, move it!" Mrs. Mallano scolds. About a hundred years old and half-blind, the golden retriever whimpers.

"Madeline!" She grabs me in a hug. I hug her back and pat Casey's head.

"Hi, Mrs. Mallano."

"What are you doing out of school? I haven't seen you in months! You finally dumped the momser. Well, I can't say I'm not disappointed. How about some hot apple cider? I just made some for myself."

In the kitchen, she pours me a glass of cider from a half-gallon plastic container that sits on the island. She pops it in the microwave and turns back to me. The smell of apples and cinnamon is strong and comforting. "Is something wrong? I'm about to leave for work."

I put my bag down. "I had a run-in with Justin this morning."

She is silent.

"He tried to grab me and he smelled like marijuana."

Still silent.

"You know, he was caught last time—"

"Yes, I know," she snaps.

I start at her tone. I have never heard her like this. "I just think something has to be done. He's really out of control and—"

Just then the microwave beeps. She turns around and yanks open the microwave door, touches the mug, snatches her hand back, and reaches for a potholder on the counter. She pulls out the mug with the mitt and turns back to me. "Look, Madeline, I think this is a very private matter between my son and I." Her voice sounds so different. So cold. "I'm sorry he grabbed you. That is wrong and I will speak with him. But I think—especially since you are no longer his girlfriend—that you should stay out of this and let me worry about how out of control Justin is or isn't." She clunks the mug down on the counter and some of the cider splashes onto her hand. She licks it off quickly. "I think you should go back to school."

"I still care about Justin. He's been my friend for a long time-"

"You have no idea how much pain my son is in. You, with the nice cozy family—" She stops, shakes her head, and leans against the counter, crossing her arms. "His father—we don't miss Joey. Ha! I bet you didn't expect that. Yes, Madeline. Joey wasn't a nice man. Not at all. Did you know that Justin's tears at the funeral were tears of happiness because now he wouldn't get knocked around for not cleaning the dishes properly or punched in the face for a bad mark in school?"

My shock and her harsh words hang in the air between us. I want to protest, to tell her I understand family secrets better than she thinks I do. I'm not surprised about Mr. Mallano.

I open my mouth to reply but she cuts me off.

"So, the next time you want to judge how out of control my son is, just think about what he has been through." She grabs the mug of cider and pours it out into the sink.

I hesitate at the door. I want to tell Mrs. Mallano I do understand Justin. I have been through all the drunken nights for past year. I'm not judging him—I want him to get better. I want to tell her my family is not perfect and cozy. But I say nothing.

CHAPTER 15

"Madeline? Madeline! Maddie, wake up, your sister is missing."

I open my eyes, and my mother's face is inches from mine.

"Wipe your cheek, Madeline, you were drooling." My mother gets up from the pink floral couch and smoothes out her beige wool pants. "Your sister is missing," she repeats. Her voice sounds funny, strained and high-pitched. She picks up my empty Coke can and shoots me a disgusted look.

"What? What time is it?" I'm surprised she hasn't already strangled me for drinking soda in her precious living room straight out of *Victorian Magazine*—frilly curtains, soft mauve lamp shades, and worst of all those tacky dolls you see in *Redbook* with names like Jennifer and Elizabeth.

"It's three in the afternoon. What were you doing asleep?"

"I was just—" Recovering from my run in with both Mallanos.

"She was supposed to work at the hospital today and she never showed up. So they called her house, and then they called here and left a message. That was at ten." The way my mother looks reminds me of a show I saw about lemurs on Animal Planet. This mother lemur had a sick baby who couldn't keep up with the nomadic pack. He got lost and she didn't realize it right away, so she went back to the last place she saw him and searched under every branch, tree, and rock. I cried through the whole thing but I couldn't stop watching it.

"Has she been sick? I thought maybe she was sleeping, but I went to her apartment and no one answered the door. Her car is gone too. I called the Adlers and they said they thought Michael was on duty until tomorrow morning. Something's wrong."

"Did you call her friends?"

She nods. "They haven't seen her either." She tucks a stray hair behind her ear. "By the way. The school called and wondered where you were today." I open my mouth to protest but she cuts me off. "I don't have time or energy to deal with that now. Just don't let that become habit."

I nod my head and sit up, still foggy. "You don't know if she's missing, Mom. She could be at the mall." But even I don't believe this. I know I have to tell her; especially now Barbara could be missing. "She's pregnant."

My mother looks at me as if I'm speaking an alien language. "Pregnant?"

"Yeah, and last night she was sitting in the TV room drinking beer and smoking at two in the morning. She doesn't want to have the baby, and she knows she has a problem."

"What are you talking about?"

"When are we going to stop pretending about Barbara? She's a drinker! She has a problem." I pause and then add, "Just like Bubbie used to."

Her eyes widen. "Oh, my God!" She crumples onto the sofa and starts to weep.

I have never seen my mother cry. I sit awkwardly next to her. When I pat her arm gently, she hugs me tight. The smell of Tresor stings my nose.

"Oh, God." My mother shakes her head as if she can shake the truth away.

It's nine o'clock in the evening. In the living room, which has French doors that open to the kitchen, my father speaks quietly to Michael, who arrived at six. Mom, Michael's parents, Mr. and Mrs. Adler, and Peter's parents, the Shaws, sit in the kitchen at the table. My mother sips tea while Mrs. Adler speaks gently to her. The white cordless phone rests next to my mother's saucer. Every few minutes we all stop and stare at it, hoping it will ring. It rang once, about two hours ago, but it was only the delivery person with the sandwiches Mrs. Shaw ordered for us all. The guy was lost. My mother could only hand the phone to my father when she realized it wasn't Barbara.

I'm not sure why my mother and I haven't told anyone Barbara is pregnant. Maybe we're hoping we will find her and she'll tell Michael. Deep down I'm afraid that she went to have an abortion. And deep down I know Barbara needs some kind of major help—not just AA. Maybe a rehab place. What really scares me is that we have no idea where she could have gone.

Michael guides me over to the wingback chairs in the corner near Mom's display cabinet of "tchotchkes," as my father calls her painted eggs collection.

"It's my fault, Maddie. I shouldn't have left her alone. Her drinking was getting so much better."

I don't know what to say to him. I pull at a cuticle and shake my head. We sit.

"Where is she, though? Why did she suddenly just take off?" Michael looks helpless and sad.

Mom walks across the pastel pink-and-blue hand-woven Persian rug and Michael stands up. "Michael, I didn't want to tell you this. I thought we would find her or she'd come home. But she's not home. I didn't realize how much she's been drinking." Mom takes a deep breath and I hold mine. "Michael, Barbara told Maddie that she's pregnant."

I exhale loudly. I can't help what I say next, looking right at Michael the whole time.

"And she was drunk when she told me. She's still drinking a lot."

Mr. and Mrs. Shaw gasp.

"What?" Mr. Adler says.

"What do you mean 'drinking a lot'?" Mrs. Adler says. She looks around at everyone. "Who doesn't have some wine every now and again?"

My father shakes his head and rubs his forehead.

"Pregnant?" Michael says with disbelief.

We all stand sadly and awkwardly for a few moments.

Then the phone rings.

CHAPTER 16

My mother rushes to the phone and picks it up. "Hello?"

We gather around her, leaning forward, hoping and praying.

"Oh, hello, Helen." It's Bubbie. My mother returns to Martha Stewart mode. "What?" A long silence follows as my mother puts her hand to her forehead.

"She's missing, Helen. We haven't seen or heard from her since Sunday morning. She took her car and clothes." Another long pause. "So you don't know exactly where she is?" My mother is exasperated. She looks at all of us with a stern expression, lips pursed, one hand on her hip. She shakes her head. "Okay. Yes, please call as soon as she calls again. Yes, we're fine. Yes, goodbye."

"I can't believe this!" My mother says. "Apparently Barbara called Helen about an hour ago and told her she was coming out to California. She took a midnight flight. She hasn't arrived yet. She called from a layover in Ohio." So Barbara did actually call Bubbie.

"Thank God!" Mrs. Adler says.

"At least we know where she is, Bern." Mrs. Shaw puts her hand on Mom's shoulder.

"Why is she going to see Helen?" my father says to no one in particular.

I take a deep breath, realizing that not only will my parents hear this, but also the Adlers and the Shaws. I just hope I'm doing the right thing. "I spoke to Bubbie a few days ago, and she told me all about the drinking problem she had and about how she thought Barbara needs help and she has thought that for a couple years." No shaking. No tears. Just playing with the hangnail on my left hand.

"Maddie, not now," Mom says with a meaningful glance at her friends.

Michael looks at me with desperate, wounded dog eyes. "Maddie, don't."

Michael is going to have to wait. I need to get to my parents first. I'm on a roll. I aim the next volley at Dad. "Bubbie said she's tried to talk to you about Barbara, and she said she thinks this all has to do with the way we treat her—like she's a loser basically—and Barbara even told me that the other night, your birthday." I pause and look at my mother. "We got into a fight."

"Madeline!" My mother has upped the volume.

My father puts his arm around my mother, who is shaking and trying to control her tears. "Maddie, we can talk about all this later."

"Actually, we really do need to get going." Mrs. Shaw grabs her black leather coat from the hall closet just off the living room. Mr. Shaw follows.

The Adlers are both red faced, and Mrs. Adler (a.k.a Chatterbox) starts rambling. "We need to go too. Herman, you know, our thirteen-year-old, diabetic cat? He needs his insulin shot. Can't wait too long. Vet says every ten hours and—" She points her to watch. "—look at the time. Nine forty-five. Need to be home by ten sharp." She bustles to the closet and grabs her mink coat and her husband's gray wool jacket. But no one can really leave yet because now I'm addressing everyone: "Anyway, Bubbie told me Barbara has to want to help herself and even though we have sort of contributed to her problem, you know, by denying it and everything—"

Suddenly all three of them—my mother, father, and Michael—start in at once:

Michael protests: "That's not true! I haven't denied anything. I've been going to Al-Anon."

"Al-Anon?" Mrs. Adler stops buttoning her coat. "What's that?"

The usually mute Mr. Adler offers, "It's for drinkers dear. I think our boy is trying to tell us that he's—"

"What?" Michael is a decibel from yelling. "No, Pop, I'm not a drinker. But my wife is."

"I resent that remark young man!" My mother purses her lips and points her finger at him. "If she's drinker, you've let her become one."

"Bern! Come on. Michael has been a wonderful man to Barbara. Don't say that. You're just upset—" My father says.

"Yes, yes I'm. And now she's pregnant." She glares at Michael. "How could you get her pregnant if she's been drinking? You can't tell me that's not your fault!"

"Now you just wait a second there, Mrs. Hickman." Mrs. Adler puts her hands on her hips. "It takes two to tango."

"But just one to plant the seed!" My mother seethes.

A collective gasp echoes around the room.

I take advantage of the quiet and burst out, "This has nothing to do with Michael, Mom. This—this—" I stop and look for the right word, and all I can think of is—"shit—" Another collective gasp and the loudest is my mother's. "This shit is probably all about, like Bubbie told me, Barbara has always felt rejected. She doesn't even know her biological father, and we never really talk about that part of our family, you know?"

Now Dad protests. "But we wanted her to feel like she was part of the family. I adopted her. She calls me Dad. We love her."

My mother straightens up, tucks an imaginary stray blond hair behind her ear, and blinks back any trace of water from her eyes. Look out. Here's Martha. "This is nonsense. Madeline, you don't know what you're talking about and neither does Helen."

I continue as if my parents hadn't said a word. "I told her to call Bubbie and talk to her. I told her she needs help and Bubbie could help her. Maybe that's why she's going out there. Maybe she's trying to get help."

"Well, she certainly needs that," Martha snaps. "But I'm not sure she'll get it in California. What she needs to do is come home."

"I agree," Michael says quietly, looking at my mother. I flop on the couch, hoping someone will say, Poor Maddie, or How did you get to be so wise?

No one says anything for a moment. Embarrassed, probably, at all this dirty family linen, the Adlers finish buttoning their coats and Michael escorts them out to their Mercedes while the Shaws make my mother promise to call them the minute they hear from Barbara.

My mother takes the cordless to the couch and cradles it in her lap. My dad sits next to her. Apparently that's it for family discussion. I feel like a lone soldier on the front line. I long to call Peter. Someone I can talk to. Maybe even Sean.

❧   ❧   ❧

By 10:30 the food arrives but remains untouched by all. Michael goes home and Dad convinces Mom to go up to bed and wait until they hear from Bubbie in the morning. My parents haven't said a word to me for the past hour, and Michael kept his distance after his parents left. He spoke softly to my father. "Things have been so great between us for the past few weeks. She's been working at the hospital, helping Mom and Dad out at the store, and talking about

going back to school. She's even been painting in the study. I just don't understand." My mother remained silent, thumbing through *Victorian* magazine and
still cradling the phone.

My father nodded and said, "I don't understand this all either. I'm trying to
make sense of it." All of them just ignoring everything I had said. It made me
so sick and angry. And sad.

Around eleven, I finally leave the wingback chair I have been anchored in
for most of the night and head to bed. I hear Mensch meow at the front door.
As soon as I open it, I smell the comforting odor of burning leaves, and I sit
outside on the front steps for a few minutes. Maybe the cold will knock the
anxiety out of me. Deep swirls of purple surround the golden full moon. Hearing laughter from next door, I look between the row of trees that separates us
from our neighbors, the Clancys. Are those boys I see with Stacy, their eigh-
teen-year-old daughter? She never has parties. Usually I see her hustling into or
out of the house, clutching thick textbooks about Chaucer or Shakespeare.
Hard to imagine her hanging out with a bunch of guys. I hear a familiar laugh
and realize it's—

Sean.

It can't be. I glide across the walkway and over the top of the circular driveway, toward the trees. "Crap." Cold asphalt hits my bare feet.

Sean is wearing jeans and drinking a bottle of Evian. He's standing in front
of Stacy, who's sitting on a wicker chair, twirling a strand of her golden hair,
her back to me.

He sees me. "Madeline?" He walks to the edge of the porch, puts the bottle
of Evian on a small wicker table, and squints. "Is that you?"

I want the trees to wrap me up in their branches. I want to shrink into a
speck of dirt. I want to—

"You know the Hickmans?" Stacy says, like we're a disease. She moves to the
other side of the porch, away from him. The others murmur while he looks
back at Stacy and then at me again. "Yeah, we're old friends." Then he hops off
the porch and walks through the trees.

"Hey." He walks across the yard toward me.

Thank God I didn't change out of my jeans and into my sweats.

"Hi…uh, I was just letting my cat inside and—" I feel like an idiot, saying I
wanted fresh air. We stand looking at each other for a long moment. With anyone else, this would be awkward.

"I'm really glad you came outside." He bends down toward me and whispers. "The whole time I've been over there, I've been thinking, now which win-

dow is Madeline's room?" He smiles, giving Freddie Prinze Jr. serious competition. The vision of him at my window both thrills and scares me.

"What are you doing here?" I hope he can't see how red my face is.

"John, that guy sitting next to Stacy, is my cousin. He knows Stacy from a Psych class at Fairfield." He pauses and I'm sure he can see my heart beating. "I couldn't believe my luck when we pulled into her driveway. John begged me to come say hi to you—just so he could have a few minutes to make his move on Stacy."

So he's talked about me to his cousin? "So why didn't you?" Would I have had the guts to let him in? Answer the door?

"Because—" He glances over at Stacy and John, who are staring at us and whispering to each other.

He takes my elbow like guys do in old movies—I'm Natalie Wood and he's Robert Wagner. We sit out of sight from them, close enough that I can feel the heat of his arm grazing mine. My parents, my harsh words to them, Barbara, Justin—all seem far away.

"—because I know that you're going through a lot of stuff. I don't want to bother you." He stops and brushes a stray hair out of my eyes like it's a normal thing for a guy to do.

I feel my eyes tear up. Oh no. Not again—

Too late. This time I make sure I'm quiet and that I don't get snot on his sleeve. I put my hand over my mouth and swallow back as many tears as possible.

"See—" He wipes the tears with his fingers.

"I wish I could just fall into your arms and forget everything." I take his hand from my face and hold it for a second then let it go. I take a deep breath. "But I'm dealing with so much right now. Stuff I need to face on my own." I'm surprised how mature I sound.

We sit in silence for a moment, looking out into the yard, and he takes my hand, in a brotherly sort of way, and pats it. "Let me be your friend."

We laugh. I'm surprised I can do that tonight. He's good for me. We are silent again for a moment. I notice that the voices next door are gone. The porch is empty.

"I have an idea," Sean says. He's still holding my hand.

"What is it?" I want to let his hand go. But I can't.

"Do you want me to wait for you?"

"Wait for me?"

He lets go of my hand and looks down into my eyes.

"Because I will. I guess I've been through enough relationships to know a lot of people aren't right for me. Most girls don't get me. Don't connect to me. But with you, man, it goes way beyond all the usual sex and bullshit with girls."

Can anyone be this sincere? "Yes," I finally say. "Yes. I just don't know how long you'll have to wait."

He stands up. Then he does this sort of brotherly, funny thing. He bends down and kisses the top of my head. "I'll give you some space and time. I'll call you for the next play—I think it's *Godspell.*"

"When will that be?"

"In the spring."

I picture us holding hands—in the not-so-brotherly, sisterly way—the warm breeze blowing my long, floral skirt. The sunshine, bright against the cloudless sky and he bends down, his pillowy lips brush mine…

"That should be enough time." And I promise myself that it will be.

I watch Sean walk back across the yard to Stacy's. Then I go inside and immediately fall asleep.

CHAPTER 17

In the morning, I feel a weird happiness about Sean's visit. He is a really good guy, and I'm not going to run to him and use him as my rebound. I want to wait until I'm definitely over and done with Justin. Something tells me we still have some unfinished business.

I take the picture of Barbara and me out of the drawer and put it back where it was. I wish I could have said the right thing to her that night I found her crying. I wish I could have made her feel better and made her tell Michael she was pregnant and scared. But would it have made a difference? No. Probably not.

In my robe, I shuffle down to the kitchen. My mother has on her light blue silk robe and nightgown. She clutches a white coffee mug, ignoring the dry toast in front of her. My father has on jeans and sneakers and a gray, stained sweatshirt. Barbara would razz him for this. "Mom's not taking you out like that!" she'd say. But Martha seems to be M.I.A.

I say nothing to either of them.

"Hi, Maddie." Dad takes a swig of coffee.

My mother gets up. "Hi, sweetie. Do you want some breakfast? I'll get you some toast."

What's this? Now they are talking to me? Being nice to me? Afraid to lose another daughter?

"No. I'll get something." With my head in the refrigerator, I ask, "Did we hear anything yet?" I keep my voice firm, businesslike.

"No."

The phone rings, the way it would in a movie.

My mother presses the answer button. "Hello?"

A long silence. Mom starts to cry and my father grabs the phone.

"Barbara? Oh, Helen. What's going on?" With his free arm, he hugs my mother, who is still crying.

His eyes on mine, he listens to Bubbie. "So, okay. Okay, yes. I think that's a good idea. We should all go, but Michael should really go now…Okay, good idea. I'll call him…Yes, then he'll call you."

My mother, by now, is amazingly calm. "She's okay. She's at Bubbie's and really wants to just sleep and relax. She doesn't want any of us to come out yet. But Bubbie convinced her to talk to Michael about the pregnancy and to let him come out there. Do you think she feels safer there than here?" She doesn't look at Dad when she asks this. She's looking at me.

"I think so." I tell her. And my mother nods.

❦   ❦   ❦

Around five o'clock, my father goes to get us some Chinese food. The Shaws are coming for dinner, and I really want Peter to show up. I took a chance and got a large Moo Shu Chicken when my dad phoned in the order. Peter and I usually share this. In my room, I dial the private number that goes right into Peter's room.

He picks up on the first ring. I can hear classical music in the background. He must be doing his geometry homework. He read somewhere that listening to Mozart can make you smarter.

"Peter? It's Maddie." I try to sound relaxed. I keep thinking if I act like everything is cool between us, maybe it will be.

"Oh, uh, hello." So formal. I guess he's still mad.

"I'm calling to see if you're coming over tonight for dinner with your parents. You can bring Susan. Is she there?" Even though I'm not quite ready to deal with Susan, I'm trying hard to be cordial.

"We broke up, so she wouldn't be here."

"Oh! I'm so sorry. Are you okay? Did this just happen?"

"Yesterday. But I'm fine." His voice sounds the way he looks when he is picking poppy seeds off a bagel. He hates poppy seeds.

A long silence and then I say, "Peter, I'm so sorry. I was really mean and just crazy. I really want to be okay with you and everything."

Another long silence. "You were pretty nasty to me."

"Yes, I was," I agree.

"And I just wanted to be there for you—"

"I know. I couldn't—"

He doesn't let me finish. "But I know Susan and I—both of us were really insensitive to what you were going through. We were pretty caught up in each other."

Really? "Yeah," I say, "but I wasn't really overjoyed and happy for the two of you, and I should have been. I know this sounds weird, but I felt left out."

"Well, you could have joined us—"

"Very funny. No thanks."

The tension deflates. I feel the way I used to feel with Peter. "So Susan and you are over? You know, I should apologize to her. I've really blown her off. I just couldn't put up with her Susanness."

He turns the music down. "Yeah, I know all about that."

"So, what...?"

"We ran out of things to do," Peter says. "We didn't have anything to say to each other. All this built-up tension between us, you know. Sort of like you and Justin. We all had this sexual tension for years and then—boom! You find out about it, and, well, we actually did it. Then we just didn't know what to do. It's pretty hard to go back to being friends. Very awkward. So we've agreed to stay away from each other for a while. She may be going to boarding school next semester. She got into Concord Academy. Her dream."

"Really?" So many changes.

Then, I ask him the question I've been dying to ask since I found out. "So...was it any good?"

"Was what any good?"

"You know..."

"The sex?" He chuckles. "Uh, yeah, what do you think? But it was also really weird, and actually I'm not ready for all that."

I can't believe a boy would ever admit this, even Peter.

He changes the subject. "You should call Susan, though. You guys were pretty tight before all this."

"I know. I'm going to call her. But first things first. Are you coming over?"

"Of course. Moo Shu chicken?"

"I already ordered it."

❋   ❋   ❋

At dinner Peter and I gorge ourselves on Moo Shu chicken and giggle about adding "in bed" to the fortunes in the fortune cookies. "You will meet many new friends...in bed." The grownups are so engrossed in their discussion about the plans for going to California to notice us. Mrs. Shaw will water the plants while we're gone and feed Mensch. Mr. Shaw offers to drive us to the airport.

The Adlers call to tell us Michael has already left. My mother actually spoke to Bubbie and called her "Mom" once. Both good signs. But I think the hardest part is going to be when Barbara and my parents see each other.

Wednesday morning at school I sit with Peter at lunch. When I pass Susan in the hallway, she looks really pissed off. Now what? We have a final meeting for this semester of the dance club and all members have to attend. When I get to the cafeteria, Susan is at a table by herself, and I decide this is the perfect opportunity to apologize.

"Hey," I say, as I pull out the chair next to her.

She stares straight ahead. "Hello."

"How have you been?" I ask awkwardly.

"How do you think?" she responds sharply, still refusing to face me.

"Well, I don't really know." What is going on?

Finally, she looks me in the eye. "Now everything is the way you want it. You were miserable and now you've spread that all around. Now we're all miserable."

"What are you talking about?"

"Maddie, don't play dumb. You know Peter and I broke up."

I feel defensive. "What does that have to do with me and my misery?"

"Didn't you want us broken up? I know you couldn't stand that we were happy, that Peter was actually happy, even without you around all the time."

"Susan, I really don't understand."

"Come on. Get real. You know what I'm talking about. Peter and I were so happy, and you and Justin were a mess. We even tried to include you and make you feel better, but that wasn't good enough for you. You wanted us miserable, just like you." She grabs her bag off the table. For a minute I think she might hit me. "You were jealous of our happiness. And you were jealous I was the one making Peter happy and you weren't."

"Hey!" Here I am trying to make amends and move on, and she's attacking me. "You know, first of all, Peter is my friend. I have never liked him in the way you are implying. And second of all, I came over here to apologize for the way things have been between us. I came over here to tell you that I missed you—"

"Please! Don't give me this missing-you crap. You don't miss me! You are so psyched Peter and I broke up. You're so glad I am out of the picture, because you've always had to have the focus on you and when it stopped being on you,

you got mad. And Peter, because he's so in love with you—don't pretend you're surprised—he felt so bad for you with Justin and everything that we fell apart." She pauses for a breath and plunges on. "Don't pull this missing-me crap, because you are so happy you don't have to deal with me anymore. I'm not in the way of you getting to Peter." She stands up so fast she knocks over her chair. "You know what? Take him. You deserve each other. But just remember, I was his first."

CHAPTER 18

After Dance Club I slide into a booth at the Coffee Connection, where Peter and I agreed last night to meet. He arrives moments after I order two lattes.

"You look terrible." Like our cat Mensch when he came home from the hospital after he'd been "fixed"—head, eyes, body, drooped and slumped.

"You don't look so great either." He takes his glasses off and rubs them on his shirt. "I ran into Susan. What's your excuse?"

"Same."

"I saw her walking home," he says. "I said hello and she gave me a I-hope-you-rot-in-hell look. Then she said something weird. It was really out of the blue."

"What?"

"'You're in love with Maddie.' And she thinks that's the real reason we broke up." He pushes up his glasses and slumps even further into the red booth. "Can you believe her?"

I don't say anything right away. I feel sort of sorry for Susan. I was angry when she yelled at me, but I think I understand. She's hurt.

"I saw her at the meeting, and she said the same thing to me. She also said I spread misery around." I grab a napkin from the dispenser on the table. "Apparently she hates me." I shred the napkin into tiny pieces. I know I'm feeling sorry for myself, but I feel sort of guilty about Susan. Was she right? Did I want to spread my misery?

"That makes both of us. She saw us this morning at your locker, so she knows we made up." He shakes his head, takes the shreds, balls them up, and puts them in a neat row. "But I don't get it. When we broke up, she said she hoped some day we would all be friends again. And our breakup was mutual. Why is she so mad?"

We are both silent. Me shredding another napkin and Peter balling up the shreds. What a pair.

Just then the nose-pierced, spiked-collar-wearing waitress, whose black roots are way too visible in her fuchsia hair, arrives with the lattes. She wordlessly slams them down. After she leaves, we both burst into giggles.

"Nose ring infection?" I whisper.

"Yeah, she badly needs to itch inside there—"

"Right. But her boss—"

"—who's sixteen—"

"—caught her scratching up in there one time and yelled at her, 'cause you can't pick your nose unless you wash your hands after"

We are both cackling like two evil witches over a boiling cauldron.

"There's—" My stomach hurts from laughing. I can't breathe. "—there's even a sign in the employee bathroom: No nose picking unless you wash hands thoroughly before returning to work."

I think I have just about peed my pants. We both guffaw until we're practically on the floor. We're in fifth grade giggling—just like this—during the spelling bee because Marcus Silvia just ripped a big, loud, smelly fart right next to barely-five-feet Ms. Brown—who we later learned was a former nun as well as a lesbian. She was so grossed out that she ran out of the assembly, holding both her nose and stomach, and we didn't see her until the following day.

Finally the laughing dies down and we're back to reality.

"Well." I dump a bunch of sugar into the white mug. "She hates us both."

"The waitress?" Peter looks around for Ms. Nose Ring. At least he's not slumping anymore.

"No. Susan. I'm talking about this whole Susan-thing." I slam my spoon into the latte and stir it like a lunatic. I'm angry at Susan and myself. I should've said something else to her—No, I didn't want you guys to be miserable. Or I just wanted someone to feel sorry for me. I also think I would have liked to say. You're just jealous of my friendship with Peter. You've always been jealous—

"Oh. Yeah. Susan." He's stirring his latte like a madman but hasn't put anything in it. I almost start laughing again, but the thought of Susan stops me.

"I bet she got jealous when she saw us this morning." I stop stirring. "I bet she never liked how close we were. She was happy when I was busy taking care of Justin, because—Guess what?—it got in the way of you and me. She knew you didn't like how Justin was acting, and I was going to stand by him. She loved that we weren't on the same page about it." I take a loud sip from my latte. Peter is still stirring and slops some coffee out. He mops the liquid up with a bunch of napkins until the table's clean enough to make even my mom proud. He stops wiping and stares at me, eyes wide, not touching his drink. I call this his Chicken-Little/The-Sky-Is-Falling-look.

"Oh, no," I say. "Did you forget to get your favorite J Crew sweater back from Susan?"

"No. I made sure I got that back before we broke up." He puts the wet napkins on the side of the table. "You don't think she's right about us, do you?"

"What do you mean? That we have the hots for each other? I hope not, considering you're looking at me like I'm the Bride of Frankenstein."

His face relaxes into a laugh. Finally, he dumps some sugar into his mug and drinks some coffee. "Maddie?"

"What, Chicken Little?"

"Very funny." He pauses. "I don't know if I ever told you this, but when Justin told me he liked you—he wanted to be your boyfriend—I was jealous." He says this like he's admitting to a grand larceny.

"Yeah, so what?" I slurp some coffee. "When Susan told me she slept with you, I was jealous. I felt like the betrayed wife—like Dixie on *All My Children* when Tad slept with Liza, his former girlfriend from high school—"

Peter's face is apple red. I choke on my latte, realizing what I have just admitted.

"You were?"

I blow my nose on a napkin to give me time to regain my composure. "That's normal, don't you think?" I ask. "We're best friends but we also happen to be a guy and a girl. Anyway, I wasn't jealous because I wanted to do it with you or anything."

"Yeah." He nods. "Me either." But Chicken Little has not left the building. Oh, no. Life is already complicated enough.

"Look," I say with finality. "Susan's mad right now because you guys just broke up." I pause. "The truth of it all is that I just wanted you guys to feel sorry for me a little. I didn't want the two of you to sit with me night after night, cry, and write bad poetry. I needed you. But I realize that you probably needed me too."

Finally, Chicken Little has left the building with the Bride of Frankenstein.

"Let's go back to being best friends," I tell Peter. "I really missed you."

CHAPTER 19

It's late in the afternoon. Must be around three or four. The sun is bright in the cloudless sky, but it feels about forty degrees. The fifteen-minute walk from the coffee shop gives me time to replay my afternoon with Peter. I never realized until today that not only do I need him, but he needs me. That we are good for each other and not in the stupid, girl-needs-boy or boy-needs-girl way. But as two friends. I smile the whole way home, kicking a rock like a soccer ball—something I don't think I've done since I was eight.

As I walk down the driveway to the house, I see that the living room windows are open. Dad must have been attempting to cook again. Probably burned some cookies or a pie. He likes to cook desserts, but they aren't exactly his forte. I overhear my parents talking in the kitchen. About me? I pause on the steps to the side door. No, about Barbara.

"Barbara never felt like she was your daughter. Don't you think?"

"No, I really don't, Bernice. I always treated and loved her like my own flesh and blood. And I am her father. I adopted her. Let's not keep trying to find someone to blame for all this."

"I know. I know. I'm sorry. Barbara never talks about Jim. She hasn't asked me about him since she was five."

It's the first time I have ever heard Barbara's bio-dad's name. The cool air nips at my bare hands. I rub them together and try not to make any noise sitting down on the steps.

"You know what I think has been a big mistake? All these years, we've expected her to be a failure. She was always so needy. Sleeping on the floor in our bedroom until she was eight. I think there's some truth to this idea of feeling abandoned by her biological father. And I think we fostered it."

What? I stop rubbing my hands and lean close to the open window, which is less than a foot from the steps.

"You do?" Mom sounds tearful.

"Yes. And then Maddie came along. Barbara had to share our attention." My dad sounds so serious. It's hard to picture. I bet he's pressing his hands together like he does when he gives lectures.

I hear pans banging together and the rustling of paper. The water from the faucet turns on and off. Mom must be cleaning up Dad's baking disaster. Dad's probably trying to wipe flour off his face.

I hear my mother's shoes click across the floor. A cabinet opens and closes. "She was always jealous."

Yeah, true. Every time I got a Barbie doll or new clothes, Barbara would cry and complain that no one ever got her presents.

Dad sighs. "How about when Maddie had diarrhea all over the brand new Toyota, and we missed half of that play Barbara was in. What was it called?"

"*A Thanksgiving Day to Remember*," Mom says. "Barb wore this little pilgrim outfit that we made together."

My parents are both laughing, but it's not the big belly laugh I usually hear from Dad or the short choppy giggles from Mom. I've heard the story a million times. Barbara was so upset our parents hadn't arrived that when it was her turn to speak her one line, she ran onstage and yelled, "My parents aren't here. I'm not acting!" Then she sat down in the middle of the stage. She was ten. It's so sad to picture that. I never realized how awful she probably felt.

My mother goes on with the story, not laughing now. "I can still see her when we finally arrived, can't you?"

"In the corner of the dressing room." My father sighs. "With her hands folded and all the teachers yelling at her for ruining the show."

"God, she was devastated," Mom says.

I'm practically glued to the side of the house. I hear more pots being moved around.

"Did you know about the drinking?" It's so weird to hear my mother say that. I wish I could see her face. Are her lips pursed Martha style? Is she biting her lower lip in concern?

"Bern, I don't think my head's been up my ass for the past ten years. I honestly never thought she had a problem. I thought, well, some kids take awhile to grow up. She's a late bloomer."

"I knew," my mother says quietly. "Not that she was an alcoholic—I still can't believe that—but I knew she couldn't handle liquor well. Remember Maddie's Bat Mitzvah?"

Oh my God, they knew!

"Of course I remember," my father says.

My mother sounds angry for a moment. "Michael tried hard to cover that one up."

"He probably thought he was protecting her. I can understand that."

They are quiet again. I feel tears spilling down my cheeks.

"Are you nervous about seeing Helen?" my father asks.

"I don't want to talk about it." Mom snaps into Martha mode. I hear her heels click across the floor toward the stairs.

I move away from the side of the house, wiping the tears away. I can't believe how selfish I've been. I'm not the only one feeling bad around here. I want to climb in my oak tree and cry. But not for myself. For my parents and Barbara.

On the street, a figure approaches our driveway. It's Justin. What is he doing here? My heart beats faster and my hands start to shake. He pauses to pull up his baggy jeans, run a hand over his black hair. Now he sees me and our eyes lock. Hatred, love, frustration, and desire wash over me. I adjust my navy sweater and bite my lip.

About four feet away, close enough for me to see the curtain of black lashes covering his blue eyes, he pauses again.

"Justin," I say.

He says nothing.

"What are you doing here?" I ask.

"I wanted to see you." His tone implies we are still together.

"Why?" I put my hands on my hips to stop the shaking.

"To apologize for being an asshole on Monday," he says.

"And every other day before that?" I spit back at him.

I fold my arms and take a step backward.

"You know what? I'm sick of this holier-then-thou crap." He steps forward. "What the hell were you thinking going to my mother and ratting on me? Now, I have to go to fucking boarding school. I may be an asshole but you're a nosy—"

He's getting loud and the windows are still open. I stomp over to him and grab his arm. "Shut up Justin. I don't need my parents to hear this, okay?" I push him down the driveway. "Listen, we can have it out. God knows I've been waiting for this. But I don't want my parents—"

He yanks his arm away from me. "So we have to protect your perfect parents but my mother has to know everything? Jesus, you told her that I grabbed you and shit. What the hell is your problem?" A loud slam quiets us for a moment. Good. Dad shut the windows. Does he know I'm out here with Justin? Did he hear any of this?

Justin turns his back to me and runs his hands through his hair. I hate how much I still want to kiss him.

"I told myself I wasn't going to do this," he says. "But you make me so mad sometimes. You always have to be right, and I always have to be wrong. I always have to be the asshole." He turns around and looks down at me, jamming his hands in his pockets.

I don't know what to say. He's right.

"I'm sorry." Finally, I look right into his eyes. "I'm sorry for telling your mother about everything. And for hitting you. I shouldn't have done that."

He doesn't say anything. He's got his I'm-trying-to-look-like-I-don't-give-a-shit look. But his eyes give him away. He looks like he did right before we kissed the first time. Like he could see through me.

I take a step toward him. "You're right." I can't help it. A tear rolls down my cheek. "You're right. I need to mind my own business." More tears.

His arms start to move like he's going to hug me, but then he lets them drop. "Don't cry. It's only boarding school. It's not prison. That's where she'd like to send me." I see the hint of a smile. I nod my head because I'm crying too much and trying to wipe each tear as it falls.

"Don't cry, Maddie."

Then we stare at each other in a really unsafe way. He reaches out to my face and wipes some tears with his thumb. Then he pulls me to him, and we hug for a few moments. Although this is probably not a good idea, I can't help but want just a slice of the old moments I had with Justin: to have his body close and breathe in that familiar, fabric softener smell, and, just for a few minutes, have it be like it was before Justin started to drink, before Barbara went AWOL, before everything changed.

So I bury my head in his shoulder and let him run his hands through my hair. I'm afraid to look up. Afraid to let go of him. I feel wetness on my neck where he has put his face, and I know he's crying too.

CHAPTER 20

❀

We fly to California just days after Bubbie brings Barbara to the rehab center in San Francisco. Michael is out there already, staying at Bubbie's. Barbara is a mess. She had a miscarriage, ironically, the first night in the hospital. The doctors said that it wasn't because of the drinking or smoking. Essentially there had never been a baby. It had never formed. All that formed was the sack the baby would have lived in. She would have had this miscarriage no matter what. She is in no shape to see anyone, but we are on our way. After an almost silent plane ride, we go from the airport straight to the center. Barbara is in the hospital part because she is getting sick. Bubbie said that Barbara had been drinking for four days straight when she arrived in California. So she is sort of "detoxing".

The hospital section of the rehab center doesn't smell like medicine or rotting bodies the way I thought it would. We take the elevator to the fourth floor. My father, hands folded in his professorlike way, rocks back and forth, heels to toes, heels to toes. My mother takes her compact out and fixes her hair. I keep thinking I forgot to brush my teeth this morning. Mostly, I want time to stop so I don't have to face whatever we will find on the fourth floor.

Barbara doesn't look like herself, more like some alternate-universe, evil-twin version. Her hair is all balled up and sticking out on the sides. She sits up in bed staring straight ahead at a muted TV, her arms folded. An IV trickles something into the back of her left hand.

"Hi, honey!" Mom, in Martha mode.

Barbara doesn't look at us. Without any emotion she says, "Please leave."

"But, sweetie, we just wanted to be here for you—"

"I told Michael and I'll tell you. I don't want any of you here right now."

I feel numb and then scared and sad. It's okay, Barbara, I want to say. We don't care if you are drinking. We're here for you.

"Just go," Barbara repeats.

That's when things get ugly.

My father strides into the room and stands right next to her bed. "We are your family. We want to help you."

Her jaw clenches and a little vein pops out on her forehead. I have seen this happen only once before, when Barbara had a heated conversation with my mother about going back to college. She turns and glares at Dad, then at Mom.

"See? I turned out just like you thought, a total loser screw up! Now you can all feel good and sorry for poor little messed-up Barbara. You can all feel good about yourselves when you stand next to me."

"Sweetie, we just want you to get better," my mother says, her voice shaky. "We love you."

"Stop pretending, Mother! You don't love me. I represent all the bad stuff, all the secrets we never talk about." She starts to cry. "Like my nasty, abusive, loser father. I bet I'm just like him, right? That's why you hate me so much?" She swipes at the tears, but they keep coming.

My mother and father have turned ashen and wide-eyed. I press my hand over my mouth so I won't cry. A nurse bustles in and bustles us out.

Bubbie and Michael are getting off the elevator. "Helen!" My father leans to kiss her cheek. "Hi, son," he says to Michael.

My mother mops her eyes with a tissue. She nods at Bubbie and lets Michael kiss her cheek.

I run to Bubbie, hug her hard, and bawl like a baby. Bubbie strokes my head.

"Hard times all around?" she asks. "Come on. Let's sit down for a minute."

The two pink couches in the waiting area remind me of our living room at home. I cry harder, wedged between Bubbie and my mother, who takes my hand. I'm sure the snot on it will disgust her, but she holds on. Looking worried, my father leans far forward in a nearby green leather chair. Michael seems unsure whether to sit or stand, go or stay. He probably wants to go see Barbara. That makes me cry harder. Go, I want to tell him.

"We're all upset, honey," Bubbie tells me. "I can imagine what she said to you all. She wasn't much better with Michael or me. "She feels ashamed and embarrassed. And angry."

"You don't hate Barbara, do you?" I ask Mom. "You're not mad at her, are you?"

"Of course not, honey!"

"Why do you hate Bubbie, Mom?" I blurt out. "Why can't you forgive her? If you can forgive Barbara, why can't you forgive Bubbie?"

My mother squeezes my hand. "I don't hate Bubbie, honey."

Bubbie looks at her. "I'm glad to hear you say that, Bernice."

I start crying again.

"But if you weren't an alcoholic, none of us would be sitting here."

I stop crying to hear Bubbie's reaction. My father wipes his face and sighs. "I think I'll get some coffee." He motions Michael to come with him. A long silence follows, while Bubbie and my mother stare each other down. Then Mom pats my hand, stands up, smoothes her dress, and wanders over to a window that looks out on a parking lot.

"I don't think that's fair." Bubbie's arm is still around me. "Barbara's drinking is not because of me or anyone else. But I don't deny that she's got the predisposition to alcoholism."

I can see Mom trying to hold herself together, maybe because I'm here. She rubs her temples. "No. Barbara's drinking isn't your fault. I'm just very upset right now."

"Okay," Bubbie says. "Well, then. Let's figure out what to do about Barbara." She pats my back, then goes to stand beside her daughter, my mother. It's a strange sight. But I like it. "She was awful to you guys, right?"

Mom nods. "She said some awful things."

"Detox is brutal on the body and the mind," Bubbie tells us. She sounds like a medical textbook. "Sometimes it exacerbates feelings that are already there. Sometimes it amplifies them."

Even though I'm not sure exactly what she means, I get the part about detox being brutal.

My father returns, bearing coffee and a Snickers for me.

"Barbara let Michael into her room. The nurse said she's letting him stay for dinner, but she doesn't want us right now."

"That's good news. She was brutal to us when we went in earlier. How are you, Stan?" Bubbie asks him.

He grimaces. "She was pretty upset in there."

We all think our own thoughts for a few minutes.

"Let's give Barbara some time tonight and come back tomorrow," Bubbie says finally. "Let's all go back to my house and get some dinner."

❧   ❧   ❧

The next morning, Barbara actually asks to see Michael and tolerates us being there too. She isn't her usually bubbly self, just polite and civil. She has her hair smoothed down, but her face is still pasty gray. She mostly talks to me, asking questions about things with my friends.

"You and Peter are better? Good, he's a good kid. I'm glad you and Justin broke up—he was a jerk." She smiles for the first time. "I knew you'd figure that out, Maddie. You're pretty smart for such a young kid." I don't know what to say, so I just reach over and hug her. Mom and Dad are standing on the other side of the bed. Dad has a dozen red roses in a glass vase. He smiles when we hug. My mother turns away and wipes her eyes with Kleenex. Barbara pats my head. After she pulls away, she turns to Dad, ignoring Mom, and says, "Thanks for the flowers." It makes me sad to see her avoid Mom. She doesn't want to see us for very long.

Barbara spends the next month in rehab, and no one can visit. Detox is not enough for an alcoholic. They need all this therapy and peace. After the rehab, Barbara stays with Bubble for four months. We never visit, but we all talk on the phone. Michael goes to stay with her a few times and brings back reports: She's going to AA everyday, she's taking yoga, she asked about you guys...

❧   ❧   ❧

I see Sean as Jesus in *Godspell*. We hang out at the cast party, which is at his house. As soon as Sean and I arrive, his sister Angie hustles up to me. She puts her arm through mine, like we are best girlfriends.

"I'm taking little Maddie on the grand tour," she calls to Sean, who is being whisked away by his fan club of actor-wannabes—a bunch of ninth-grade girls who had way too many piercings and Kool-Aid-pink dyed hair. If Sean was my boyfriend, I wouldn't be too worried.

After the twenty-minute tour of their three-level, remodeled, Victorian home—complete with a master bathroom the size of my living room and a game room with real video games—Angie starts grilling me. As we enter the party room, which is in the basement, she gushes, "Do you like my brother? He still talks about you all the time. No other girl stands a chance. He told me he was waiting for you. How long are you going to make him wait..."

Finally, I interrupt her and say, "Angie, Sean and I are friends."

"But—"

I tell her again. She starts to protest, but Sean sees us and runs right over. "It's time for Maddie to meet the cast." He steers me toward a group of people playing charades in a corner of the basement.

When he drives me home that night he walks me to the door. It is a cool April night, but I can smell the faint perfume of my mother's spring plantings as we stand on the front steps.

"So, you had a good time?"

I nod and fumble for my house key. Does he want more than a hug tonight? I find my key and look up at him. Is he still waiting for me?

"Maddie, I still think about you a lot, and I think it might be too hard for me to just be friends right now. Tonight was hard. I kept wanting to hold your hand and kiss you." He smiles and brushes a stray hair out of my face. I realize that I want to want to kiss him, but I really don't feel ready. I'm not even sure what that meant. "I know you're not ready."

I reach up and hug him. "Thanks."

"For what?"

"For understanding." I turn toward the door but hesitate and look back at him. "When you're ready Sean, to be friends, will you call me?"

He smiles. "Definitely. And when you're ready for more—"

"I'll give you a call."

❦   ❦   ❦

At first things are quiet when Barbara finally comes home. We give her a welcome-home dinner at their apartment, takeout from Marcucci's, Barbara's favorite. She and Mom are civil and polite. We all walk on eggshells.

It all blows up the next day. Barbara comes to our house to pick up some candid pictures from the wedding. My mother put together an album for her with the best shots. This is the first time Barbara has been to the house since the night I found her drunk in the den. She seems like a guest. She rings the bell, keeps her coat on, and Mom says hello. Barbara manages a clipped hi. She stands in the living room while Mom goes to get the pictures in the kitchen. "Why don't you come into the kitchen?" She calls out to Barbara. "We can sit and talk for a few minutes. I'll make some tea."

My sister freezes. I'm at the top of the stairs, on my way back from my parents' room with a bottle of Mom's good shampoo.

"Actually, Mom, I'm in a hurry."

I can practically see the tension build, like a giant hot-air balloon. Then my mother freaks out. "I don't understand all this anger you have toward me. What did I ever do except love and care for you the best I could?" Oh, boy.

Barbara's face goes ashen, and she looks scared and uncomfortable.

Mom walks over to her. "Just tell me what I did. Tell me why you're so upset with me."

Barbara says quietly, "Just leave me alone. I don't feel like talking about this right now." Can't Mom hear the warning in her voice? No.

"Barbara, we need to talk—"

My sister whirls around, her face fierce. "How come you never noticed? How come you never knew how much I was drinking? How come you never knew Maddie was getting me up most mornings or sneaking me into the house most nights?" She is screaming now, with a scary, scary fury. "How come you never, ever noticed? Were you blind?"

"I...I..." My mother's voice trembles.

"See, you have no answer. I do. You didn't notice because you didn't want to."

"No—" Mom begins.

"Yes! You refused to see I was screwed up, because if you saw it—" My sister's voice is scratchy and raw. "If you saw it, you'd realize maybe you screwed up somewhere along the way too!"

Mom is crying. I'm clutching the shampoo so hard that I'm surprised it doesn't shatter. "I'm sorry. I *really* am sorry Barbara. I never saw it. Maybe I did know—on some level. I mean, I knew you went out and went to parties." Mom's voice breaks. Barbara glares at her, not giving an inch.

Mom tries again. "I had a mother who drank, and I just couldn't believe I would have a child who...who had a problem like she did. I thought you were a little immature and going through some phase."

"A seven-year phase?" Barbara's voice drips sarcasm.

"Barbara, I swear, I never had any idea you were drinking as much as you say you were. You hid it from us, you know. You did a good job of hiding. You always worked and you always got up and functioned. Your dad and I wanted so much for you...I didn't think—"

"You've got that right. It's like I said in California—I was doomed to be a screw up because of my biological father, and you look at me—"

Mom cuts her off. "I do *not* look at you as a reminder of my past or as a reminder of your biological father. I love you. I may be critical and controlling at times, but I love you, and I don't want you to be a screw up."

Her words hang in the air like musical notes and echo in my ears. "I love you…I don't want you to be a screw up." A weird noise, like a wounded cat, comes from my sister. "I just feel so inadequate," she tells Mom. "I feel like a failure. I've always felt like that. I've always felt like that around you."

Mom closes the distance between them, and Barbara lets her hug her for a second, then pulls away. As if her bones melt, she collapses on the couch, her head in her hands. I have my fist in my mouth, holding in my own tears, so they wouldn't hear me.

My sister wipes her face and takes a deep breath. "This counselor in California always asked me what I got out of drinking. Not that alcoholics need a reason to drink, but it would help me if I could figure out what I think is missing. You know, in my life."

"What did you figure out?" Mom asks. Good. Just what I want to know.

"Mostly that I wanted attention from you. I never seem to do the right thing, and if I do, no one notices. Like when I took that art class and I got an A, and the teacher wanted me to enter some contest? You never said a word about it. But when I got arrested for shoplifting that summer, you let me have it for three hours and grounded me and watched me like a hawk. It seemed when I got attention, it was always for bad things. Maddie's the good kid, and I'm the bad one."

I grimace at the comparison.

"Maddie has her own problems." Right, I think. I'm ready for a little sympathy. "Have you ever wondered why she doesn't have even one girlfriend?" What? What is *this* about? "She's very good at minding other people's business. She thinks she's taking care of them—like with you. But a lot of people resent that kind of taking care of. We heard this saying at Al-Anon: Helping is the sunny side of control. I'm not sure Maddie heard it, though."

I'm stunned. My God. I'm a pain in the ass? I'm a self-righteous—Wait a minute. I will not have a pity party about myself. I have some issues I have to work on. How's that for not paying attention to Al-Anon?

"I always figured you wanted me to be more like her," Barbara chokes out. I always thought so too.

"Never," Mom says. "I want you to be more like you. The best you."

"But what about my—my other father? I know I look like him. It must make you sick to look at me."

Slowly, oh so softly, Mom says, "I never, ever look at you and think of him. I don't know why I'm so hard on you. Except that you have so much to offer and you seem to get in your own way. I look at you and think about all your potential and how I have failed you and how I should have worked harder to not let you be affected by my mistakes. I'm so sorry, and I'm so proud of you for getting sober. This is the greatest achievement there is."

My father appears in the study doorway with his hair all over the place, "Hey—why all the sad faces? I just found out Smack Down is coming to Stanford! Who's in?"

I come down the stairs, unsure now of where I fit in all this. But Dad grabs me, and we all start hugging and laughing and crying.

❈   ❈   ❈

Since that night, things have gotten much better, although they aren't perfect. Mom still isn't snugly and warm toward Bubbie, although she's including her in family occasions. When she arrived yesterday, my mother didn't hug her but instead awkwardly took her hand. She also still calls her Helen.

❈   ❈   ❈

The suit skirt hangs below my knees. It should be a few inches above. The waist is around my hips. Much too loose. The too-small linen jacket barely closes in the front. The gray washes me out. It's not a pleasant sight.

"Madeline?" My mother's muffled voice comes through the door. "How does it look? If you don't like it, I can take it back,"

Maybe I should show her. She'll see for herself how terrible it is, and then I won't have to hurt her feelings.

Maybe I should say I don't feel well. I do look kind of yellow.

"Can we come in?" My mother and Barbara.

They'd have to be blind not to see how terrible this is.

"Sure," I say with forced enthusiasm.

They bustle in and start oohing and ahhing.

"Oh, it's really classy!"

"So mature!"

"I love it! It's perfect!"

"I like the way it falls on you!" Doesn't she mean "*off* me"?

They pull and shift the suit, turning me around.

As grossed out as I'm by this outfit, I'm glad to see my sister and mother so giggly and happy together.

"Bern? Barb? Where's everybody?" My father hurricanes into the room with a bag of groceries. "Hey! Look at you! Wow, that's a great suit!"

Now we just need—

Bubbie and Michael, toting more grocery bags, poke their heads through the doorway.

Family reunion here.

Minutes later, everyone but Barbara leaves to begin making the Passover meal, three hours away. Barbara gives me a funny look.

"What?" I ask.

"You hate the suit."

"No, I don't hate it—"

"Yes you do!"

"No—"

She laughs. "Hey, you can tell the truth. You hate it!"

"Sshh! It's fine," I tell her, tugging on the suit jacket so I can breathe.

"Just put on that light green dress from Express you have." She grins. She goes to my closet for the dress, practically screaming. "Maddie hates the suit! Maddie hates the suit!"

My mother comes rushing down the hallway. "Do you really hate it?" She looks disappointed. "Okay," she says. "Take it off. Maybe we can go to Macy's together and get something you like. Baggy jeans?"

My jaw drops.

Later, I sit at the Passover table in—not my green dress, but a pair of baggy jeans and a flannel shirt. My hair is uncombed. My sister sits next to me in similar attire. The most surprising is my mother. She's wearing a pair of jeans (pressed) and a button-down white shirt. Of course, it is belted and she's wearing perfect gold hoops, but she's sitting next to my Bubbie, and I see her reach for her mother's hand. I reach for Barbara's and she reaches for Mom's. Dad enters the dining room, grinning like a mad scientist and carrying two five-pound, roasted chickens. Michael follows right behind, watching Dad to make sure he doesn't drop the birds.

My family. How we all need each other.

0-595-31265-9

Printed in the United States
64331LVS00005B/595-642

9 780595 312658